S0-ABD-087

"You squealin' son of a bitch!" he shouted.

The shotgun boomed loudly.

Win had no choice then. He dropped his beer and pulled his pistol, firing just as the man at the top of the stairs squeezed his own trigger. Win and Joe had jumped in opposite directions just as the man fired. The heavy charge of buckshot tore a large hole in the top and side of the bar, right where the two brothers had been standing . . .

DON'T MISS THESE
ALL-ACTION WESTERN SERIES
FROM THE BERKLEY PUBLISHING GROUP

THE GUNSMITH by J. R. Roberts
Clint Adams was a legend among lawmen, outlaws, and ladies.
They called him . . . the Gunsmith.

LONGARM by Tabor Evans
The popular long-running series about U.S. Deputy Marshal
Long—his life, his loves, his fight for justice.

SLOCUM by Jake Logan
Today's longest-running action Western. John Slocum rides a
deadly trail of hot blood and cold steel.

BUSHWHACKERS by B. J. Lanagan
An action-packed series by the creators of Longarm! The rous-
ing adventures of the most brutal gang of cutthroats ever assembled—Quantrill's Raiders.

BUSHWHACKERS

Epitaph

B. J. Lanagan

JOVE BOOKS, NEW YORK

If you purchased this book without a cover, you should be aware that this book is stolen property. It was reported as "unsold and destroyed" to the publisher, and neither the author nor the publisher has received any payment for this "stripped book."

EPITAPH

A Jove Book / published by arrangement with
the author

PRINTING HISTORY
Jove edition / June 1998

All rights reserved.
Copyright © 1998 by Jove Publications, Inc.
This book may not be reproduced in whole
or in part, by mimeograph or any other means,
without permission. For information address:
The Berkley Publishing Group, a member of Penguin Putnam Inc.,
200 Madison Avenue,
New York, New York 10016.

The Penguin Putnam Inc. World Wide Web site address is
http://www.penguinputnam.com

ISBN: 0-515-12290-4

A JOVE BOOK®
Jove Books are published by The Berkley Publishing Group,
a member of Penguin Putnam Inc.,
200 Madison Avenue, New York, New York 10016.
JOVE and the "J" design are trademarks
belonging to Jove Publications, Inc.

PRINTED IN THE UNITED STATES OF AMERICA

10 9 8 7 6 5 4 3 2 1

BUSHWHACKERS

Epitaph

1

WHEN THE SOLDIERS HAPPENED ACROSS B. J. MORGAN IN THE Dragoon Mountains of southeastern Arizona Territory, he looked like the sole survivor of some lost tribe of savages. His long black hair was matted and stringy on his shoulders, his beard was a nest of crawling things, and his clothes were filthy and patched with rabbit skin. The soldiers had to look a second time before they realized that he was a civilized member of their own society.

"What the hell are you doin' out here?" the sergeant in charge of the patrol asked.

"I'm prospectin'," Morgan answered.

"Prospectin'? Ha!" the sergeant laughed. "Prospectin' for what?"

"For whatever I can find," Morgan said. "I aim to leave my mark on this country."

The sergeant laughed again. "Mister, the only mark you're going to leave here is the mark they put on your tombstone. Your epitaph."

The soldiers rode on, leaving B. J. Morgan to poke around the hills alone. A short time later he discovered silver-bearing ore, and not just in some small amount, but in huge veins that stretched for thousands of yards back into the mountains. A town sprang up on the desert bedrock around the silver hills, and B. J. Morgan, remembering the sergeant's derisive comment, decided to call the town Epitaph.

•   •   •

Joe Coulter's first impression of Epitaph was one of incredible heat. It bore down on him like some great weight. He stood on the station platform while behind him vented steam from the train's escape valve sounded like some exhausted monster, gasping for breath in the terrible heat. Heat waves shimmered up from the streets and Joe wondered what kept the town from melting.

Joe's brother, Win, had gone forward to check on the horses, who had ridden in the stock car.

Joe saw a black frying pan sitting on a stump and he walked over to pick it up. The handle of the skillet was as hot as if it had been sitting over an open fire, and with a sharp exclamation of pain he dropped the pan.

Three or four of the town's citizens were sitting on a baggage cart under the shade of the car shed's overhang. When they saw Joe's reaction, they all burst out in loud guffaws.

"Was the pan hot, mister?" one of them asked.

"Not really," Joe answered, managing a good-natured grin despite his embarrassment.

"It wasn't? Why, you sure put it down fast," another of the men said.

"Well, hell, how long does it take to look at a pan?" Joe asked.

"How long does it take to look at a pan?" the man replied, and he and the others laughed loudly at Joe's rejoinder. "That's pretty good. We've caught lots of folks with that skillet, but you been the best yet. Mister, you're all right in our book."

"Why do you keep this skillet sitting out here like this?" Joe asked.

"Well, since you been such a good sport about it, I'll tell you the truth," one of the men said. "We're trollin' for fools."

"What?"

"You got any idea how hot a black iron skillet like that can get in this sun? Well, you do now, you picked it up. But there's lots of folks who are just as curious, and if you'll excuse me for sayin' so, just as much a fool as you were.

They can't keep their hands offen it. They walk over and pick it up, and we get our little laugh. Like I say, we're trollin' for fools.''

"Let me show you somethin', mister,'' one of the others said. He picked up an egg and brought it over to the pan, then broke it. The egg began to sizzle and turn white.

Joe chuckled. "There must not be a hell of a lot to do in Epitaph if you have to stay down here and do this,'' he said.

"Oh, I wouldn't say that. Problem is, Epitaph don't really come to life till it's dark.''

Win came up to join his brother.

"The horses made the trip just fine,'' he said.

"Where are they?''

"I've already made a deal to have them put up at the corral.'' He saw Joe holding his hand. "What happened to your hand?''

"Nothin'. Hey, Win, do you see that skillet over there, sittin' on the stump?'' Joe asked.

Win glanced over. "Yeah, I see it. What about it?''

"Looks like a pretty good skillet to me. Someone must've left it there. Why don't you go get it?''

"That would be a damn fool thing to do, don't you think? I mean, to pick up a black iron skillet that's been sittin' in the sun all day.''

Joe looked over at the men who had caught him with the trick, and they smiled at him.

"Yeah,'' Joe said, still rubbing his hand. "Yeah, that would be pretty much of a fool thing to do, all right,'' he agreed.

Although he was the older of the two brothers, Win was the smaller. He was about five feet, eight inches tall, with ash-blond hair and the hard face and seasoned blue eyes of someone who had seen more than his share of hard times. Joe was six foot one, with broad shoulders, and darker hair. Anyone could see that Joe was Win's brother, if they happened to look into his eyes. They were the duplicate of Win's, and they measured life with the same reserved scrutiny. But the similarity stopped. Joe was a powerful man whose first solution to any problem was his strength. Win had a wiry toughness about him, but his greatest strength was in his wits and quickness. Both men made formidable enemies and neither was a stranger to the gun, should the situation reach that extreme.

Win and Joe Coulter were in the Arizona Territory, having arrived there in a casual westward drift that neither proposed a particular destination nor had a sense of purpose. The brothers hailed from Missouri, but years of bloody border war as members of Quantrill's Raiders had set them on their wandering. They were called Bushwhackers then and still thought of themselves in such terms. Their wartime activity had earned them a degree of notoriety and, like Frank and Jesse James, the Younger brothers, and others who had ridden with them during the late war, they were now regarded as outlaws and their pictures could occasionally be found on old reward posters in Missouri, Kansas, Arkansas, Louisiana, and even in parts of Texas.

At the end of the Civil War, millions of soldiers who had worn the blue and the gray laid down their arms and picked up where they had left off. Friendships were renewed, crops were put in, men and women were married, children were born, and their lives went on as if nothing had happened.

But it was not to be so for all men. For some, the wounds had cut too deeply and the price had been too dear. Families, fortunes, and dreams were consumed in flames and drowned in blood.

Win and Joe were such men. They had only each other, a dwindling number of their peers, their guns, their courage, and a peculiar though quite rigid code of honor to sustain them. For them the war had not ended. Only the battles had changed.

Leaving the depot, the two brothers walked up the wide, sun-baked street, hurrying from the shade of one adobe building to the next, taking every opportunity to get out of the sun. After a walk of a few blocks they were drenched with sweat, and the cool interior of the Red Bull Saloon beckoned them. A sign outside the saloon promised cold beer and they thought nothing could be better than that. They pushed their way through the batwing doors and went inside. It was so dark that they had to stand there for a moment or two until their eyes adjusted. The bar was made of burnished mahogany with a highly polished brass footrail. Crisp, clean white towels hung from hooks on the customers' side of the bar, spaced every four feet. A mirror behind the bar was flanked on each side by a small statue of a nude woman set back in a special niche. A row of whiskey bottles sat in front of the mirror, reflected in the glass so that the row of bottles seemed to be two deep. A bartender with pomaded black hair and a waxed handlebar moustache stood behind the bar industriously polishing glasses.

"Is the beer really cold?" Joe asked.

The bartender looked up at him, but he didn't stop polishing the glasses. "It's cooler than horse piss," he said, in a matter-of-fact voice.

"Two beers," Win said.

"And I'll have the same," Joe added. The bartender, who thought that Win had ordered for both of them, chuckled, then drew the beers and put them in front of the two brothers.

Win picked up the first beer and took a long drink before he turned to look around the place. A card game was going on in the corner and he watched it for a few minutes while he drank his beer.

The back door opened and a tall, broad-shouldered, bearded man wearing a badge stepped through the door. He pointed a gun toward the table.

"Mathis, I didn't think you'd be dumb enough to come back to Epitaph."

The man the marshal was talking to, one of the card players, stood up slowly, then turned to face the marshal.

"Yeah, well, I decided not to let any pissant of a marshal run me out."

The situation had the look of an impending gunfight, and the remaining card players jumped up from the table and moved out of the way.

"I gave you two choices. Get out of town, or spend time in my jail. Looks to me like you've made your choice," the marshal said.

"I wouldn't want to be goin' to jail," Mathis said. "Not with this here winnin' hand I got."

"Unbuckle your gun belt, slow and easy," the marshal ordered.

Mathis shook his head. "I don't think so, Corbett. I think me an' you are goin' to have to settle this thing, once and for all."

Win, like the others, was watching the drama unfold when he heard something, a soft squeaking sound as if weight were being put down on a loose board. He looked up toward the top of the stairs and saw a man standing there, aiming a shotgun at the marshal's back.

"Marshal, look out!" Win shouted. When he shouted the warning, the man wielding the shotgun turned it toward Win and Joe.

"You squealin' son of a bitch!" he shouted. The shotgun boomed loudly.

Win had no choice then. He dropped his beer and pulled his pistol, firing just as the man at the top of the stairs squeezed his own trigger. Win and Joe had jumped in opposite directions just as the man fired. The heavy charge of buckshot tore a large hole in the top and side of the bar, right where the two brothers had been standing. Some of the shot hit the whiskey bottles, the mirror, and one of the nude statues behind the bar. Like shrapnel from an exploding bomb, pieces of glass flew everywhere. The mirror fell, except for a few jagged shards that hung in place where the mirror had been, reflecting twisting images of the dramatic scene before it.

Win's shot had been accurately placed; the man with the shotgun dropped his weapon and grabbed his neck. He stood there, stupidly, for a moment, clutching his neck as blood spilled between his fingers. Then his eyes rolled up in his head and he fell, twisting around so that, on his back and head-first, he slid down the stairs, following his clattering shotgun to the ground floor. He lay motionless with open, sightless eyes staring up toward the ceiling.

The sound of the two gunshots had riveted everyone's attention to the exchange, and while their attention was diverted from him, Mathis took the opportunity to go for his own gun. Suddenly the saloon was filled with the roar of another gunshot as Mathis fired at Marshal Corbett.

Corbett had made the mistake of being diverted by the gun-play between Win and the shotgun shooter. It was a fatal mistake, because Mathis's bullet struck the marshal in the forehead and the impact knocked him back onto a nearby table. Corbett lay belly up on the table with his head hanging down on the far side while blood dripped from the hole in his forehead to form a puddle below him. His gun fell from his lifeless hand and clattered to the floor. Mathis then swung his pistol toward Win. For a moment the two men stood *en tableau,* each holding a gun on the other.

"Mister, this ain't my fight," Win said.

"Wrong. You made it your fight when you kilt my pardner. Now I reckon I'm goin' to have to kill you."

While Mathis was talking, Win was acting. He pulled the trigger and his bullet caught Mathis in the center of his chest. Mathis went down, dead before he hit the floor.

"What's goin' on in here?" a voice asked. "What's all the shootin'?"

When Win turned toward the sound of the voice, he saw a man standing just inside the open door. Because of the brightness of the light behind the man Win couldn't make out his features.

"Get out of the light," Win growled.

"You don't tell me what to do, I—"

Win pulled the hammer back and his pistol made a deadly metallic click as the sear engaged the cylinder.

"Get out of the light or I'll kill you where you stand."

The figure moved out of the light. When he did, Win saw that he was wearing a sheriff's badge. He put his pistol away.

"Sheriff, I'm glad you come," one of the men who had been playing cards said. "This here fella just shot Charley Pearl and Vernon Mathis down in cold blood."

"You lying son of a bitch," Win said. "I don't know who you are but—"

"That's Deekus Taggart," the sheriff said. "He's my deputy. And if he says you kilt them two men then I'm goin' to have to take you in."

Although Win had already holstered his pistol, it suddenly

appeared in his hand again, the draw as fast as the wink of an eye.

"I don't think so, Sheriff," Win said. By now, Joe had his gun out as well, between the two of them, everyone in the saloon was effectively covered. "Now, I don't know what this man saw, or thinks he saw. But the man lying belly up on the table over there is a lawman. I didn't have anything to do with killing him. The other two were trying to kill me."

"Sheriff Bean, Taggart is the one who is lying," one of the other saloon patrons said. "This fella is telling the truth. Charley Pearl started shootin' first, usin' a scatter-gun. Take a look at the bar there and you'll see what I'm talkin' about. Then Mathis killed Corbett and swung his gun around toward this fella, tellin' him he was fixin' to kill him too. Knowin' Mathis, you got to figure that he was goin' to do just what he said. For a minute there, they had what you call a Mexican standoff. Then, this fella pulled the trigger . . . which if you ask me, he had every right to do."

"Why should I listen to you, Rawlings?" Bean asked. "Mathis and Pearl both rode for the McHenrys and ever'one knows you ain't been none too friendly with the McHenrys. And if memory serves me, you had a run-in with Mathis over a few head of cows not long ago."

"I still believe the son of a bitch meant to steal those cows," Rawlings replied. "But that has nothing to do with what happened here. I'm telling you the truth about what I saw."

"Kyle ain't lying, Sheriff," the bartender said. "Except for Deekus Taggart, you can ask anyone in here, they'll all say the same thing."

There was a general buzz of agreement from all the other patrons in the saloon.

Sheriff Bean glared at Kyle Rawlings for a moment more, then pointed at Win. "All right, I got nothing on you now," he said. "But I'll be keepin' my eye on you." He turned, and walked out.

"Sheriff, wait!" Taggart called. Looking cautiously at Win and Joe, all the while holding his hands up to show that he represented no danger to them, Taggart hurried to join Sheriff Bean in making an exit.

"I'll be damned," Win said after Taggart and the sheriff left. "They didn't seem at all concerned that another lawman was killed."

"Sheriff Bean and Deputy Taggart wasn't exactly what you'd call friendly with Marshal Corbett," the bartender explained. He drew two more beers. "My name is Sam. Sam Norton. And these are on the house," he said, sliding them across to the two brothers.

"Thanks, Sam," Win said. He looked at the young cowboy who had backed him up. "And I want to thank you, too, Rawlings, for telling the sheriff how it was."

"Think nothin' of it," Rawlings said. "Truth to tell, you prob'ly made yourself a lot of friends around here today."

"How's that?" Win asked.

Rawlings nodded toward the bodies, which were now being carried out of the saloon.

"Marshal Corbett was a good man. If it had been up to Sheriff Bean and Deputy Taggart, he would've been shot down today, and nothing would have happened to the two who did it. I reckon the townfolk are all goin' to figure justice was served."

"Why don't you tell him the rest of it, Rawlings?" Sam asked.

"Yeah, well, when word gets around about what happened, you'll wind up having made yourself as many enemies as you have friends," Rawlings said. "And the enemies you'll make—Ike Kramer and Jim and Frank McHenry—aren't the kind of enemies a man wants to have."

"Who are they?" Win asked.

"They're ranchers," Rawlings answered. "And they're dangerous men to cross."

"You see, boys," Sam continued, "what you have stumbled into is sort of a war."

"A war?"

"Yes, with the ranchers and the cowboys on one side, and

the miners and the townspeople on the other side.''

"But you're a rancher, aren't you?'' Win asked Kyle. "Which side are you on?''

"I'm on Kyle Rawlings's side,'' Kyle answered, easily.

2

FOR J. C. MALONE, THE EDITOR OF THE EPITAPH NEWSPAPER, which was fittingly enough called *The Last Word*, Win and Joe Coulter's arrival in town occurred at exactly the right time. He was just putting the day's newspaper together and what had been the lead, a story about a new smelter being installed in the Lucky Strike mine, was replaced with a story of the gunfight.

YESTERDAY'S FATEFUL EVENTS
Three Men Hurled Into Eternity
In The Blink Of An Eye

In the story that followed, the editor of *The Last Word* left no doubt as to where he stood. Although all good men of the town would lament the passing of Marshal Corbett, there would be no tears shed over the deaths of Charley Pearl and Vernon Mathis.

Seven miles from town, along the San Pedro River, Ike Kramer heard Sheriff Bean and Deputy Taggart's account of what had happened.

"Was this fella that good? Or was he just lucky?" Ike asked. He and his younger brother, Billy, owned the Kramer ranch, the largest of all the area ranches. Billy Kramer wasn't present for this particular discussion, but Ike's neighbors and closest friends, Jim and Frank McHenry, were. The McHenry brothers owned the adjoining ranch.

"I couldn't say he was all that good," Taggart said, answering the question. "The thing is, Charley wasn't expectin' a stranger to take a hand in a private fight. And then, when the stranger killed Vernon, he already had the drop on him. I seen that myself. He just up and pulled the trigger."

"Why didn't you take a hand in it?" Ike asked. "You was there."

"Yeah, well, the thing is, I didn't have no idea none of this was goin' to happen. First thing you know there was all this shootin' goin' on, and the next thing you know, this here stranger was standin' there holdin' a gun in his hand. What was I supposed to do?" Taggart said, defending himself.

"Who is he, anyhow?"

"I don't know, I never seen him before. Him and his brother just come into town, yesterday. I talked to some people who seen 'em get off the train."

"I don't like havin' people like that around," Ike said. "You're goin' to have to get rid of 'em, some way."

"Maybe there'll be no need for that," Taggart suggested. "Could be they'll move on by them ownselves if we just wait."

"*If?*" Ike asked, glaring at him. "*If* a frog had wings, he wouldn't bump his ass ever' time he jumps," he said. "We got things goin' our way aroun' here, and it'll keep on goin' our way 'long as the people in town don't get a backbone. I don't want these two men givin' 'em that backbone."

Two miles away from the house, Billy Kramer swung down from his horse and walked over to the edge of the cliff to look down into the canyon below. He was short and slim, with sandy hair and blue eyes. He wasn't wearing a gun belt, though he did have a rifle in a saddle scabbard.

The horse was pulling at the reins, trying to get to some grass, so Billy dropped them to let him nibble around the few sweet green shoots he was able to find on the rocky ledge.

"So, what do you think, Dancer? You want to go into town tonight?"

The horse chewed loudly.

"Don't talk with your mouth full," Billy teased. He walked over and patted Dancer affectionately on the neck. "Too bad they don't have any mares boarded at the Jingle Bell Corral," he said. "If they did, you could have some fun there while I'm over at the Courtesan House. I ought to tell Muley that. He could get some brood mares brought in, and the Jingle Bell Corral could become a whorehouse for horses." He laughed out loud. "Yeah," he said. "I like that idea. A whorehouse for horses."

Billy swung into the saddle and started back toward the house. He had heard Ike say earlier that he was going into town also. He just hoped that Ike would stay out of trouble tonight. He loved his brother, but Ike was very hot tempered, and when he got drunk, which was often, he could be a major pain in the ass.

Although the Kramer ranch and the McHenry ranch were the two biggest ranches in the county, theirs weren't the only ranches. There were at least half a dozen others, including the Rawlings spread. Kyle Rawlings, who once rode for Ike and Billy Kramer, had realized the dream of every cowboy by starting his own ranch. A small ranch as local ranches went, it was wedged in, like a piece of pie, between the Kramer place and the McHenry spread. The large end of the pie-shaped wedge was bordered by the river. And, while the river frontage made Kyle's ranch feasible, that same frontage was also a thorn in Ike Kramer's side. Ike reasoned that he could increase the size of his herd by twenty-five percent if he had the river frontage that now belonged to Kyle Rawlings.

What made Kyle's possession of the land even more difficult for Ike Kramer to swallow was the fact that the land had once been Kramer land. He and Billy had given it to their sister, Sally, so she could build a house there, when she got married.

But Sally was a homely woman who, even with her land, was unable to catch the eye of a suitor. And although Kyle never actually paid court to Sally, he did treat her kindly and Sally remembered that. When she died of some undiagnosed malady, Ike, Billy, and most of all Kyle were surprised to discover that Sally Kramer had left her land and all her possessions to Kyle Rawlings.

Billy had passed it off, saying that it had been Sally's land to do with as she saw fit, but Ike was angry about it and went to a lawyer to try and break the will. There was nothing he could do to break the will as it stood, but there was a codicil to the will that stated that Kyle Rawlings must work the ranch for ten consecutive years, or the land would return to her brothers.

In one day Kyle Rawlings went from being a rider for Ike Kramer to the biggest thorn in his side. It was not a situation Ike accepted easily; he did everything he could to make it difficult for Kyle, hoping to force him off before he had fulfilled the ten years required by the will.

To that end, he let it be known that any cowboy who rode for Kyle would never again be able to ride for him. He undersold Kyle in the cattle market and he booked more cattle cars than he needed, thus denying Kyle rail transportation. He also let his cattle graze on Kyle's land and urged Jim and Frank McHenry to do the same thing, in order to thin Kyle's grass.

Because Kyle had the smallest ranch in the county, in terms of acreage and size of herd, he did not feel that the ranchers' dispute with the townspeople had anything to do with him. But, because he was a rancher and not a town merchant, neither did he ally himself with the town. The result was that in the quarrel between the ranchers and the town, Kyle neither took a side nor did he have an ally.

On the Rawlings ranch, Kyle sat on a stone outcrop and leaned back against a boulder. Though literally as hard as a rock, the seat felt comfortable to him because it was the first time he had been off a horse in several hours. His legs hurt and his seat was sore and he was so tired he could stretch out right here and go to sleep.

Slim, his foreman, brought him a skillet of beans and bacon.

There were a couple of biscuits and an onion slice on the side.

"Uhmm, biscuits?" Kyle said.

"They can't no one make biscuits to compare with Slim's, not even that Mex cook Maggie DeShay has at that fancy whorehouse she runs," Parker, one of the drovers, said. "Boss, I tell you, Slim is gonna make some hard-drivin' woman an awful good husband," he teased. "Hell, come to think of it, I might even marry him my own self."

Parker and the others guffawed and Slim, who was emptying the last dregs of a cup of coffee, threw the rest toward the man who was teasing him. It was all in good fun, though, with little chance of an actual fight erupting. There were four men sitting around the fire and two more out riding night herd. Those six represented Kyle's entire outfit. The fire had just about burned down and was little more than glowing embers.

"Boss, I throwed your roll down over here," Leroy said. Nearly sixty, Leroy was by far the oldest of the drovers and was sort of the father figure to all of them. "It's on high ground 'n' 'bout as level as anyplace I could find around here."

"Thanks, Leroy," Kyle said as he raked his biscuit through the last of the bean juice. He dunked his kit in a bucket of water, cleaned it off with some sand, then folded it and put it away.

The other men had all ridden for other spreads before they came to work for Kyle. Kyle wasn't able to pay them the same wages the other ranchers could, but he offered them something more. He offered them a share in the herd. He would keep the land for his own, but he promised his cowboys that they would share in ownership of the herd. That arrangement had created binding loyalties and strengthened friendship. Kyle's ranch might be the smallest in the county, he reasoned, but everyone who worked there believed it was, by far, the best place to be.

When the men who worked for Kyle encountered the hands from the other ranches in town they sometimes teased them for being *cowboys*, while they, by virtue of their joint ownership of the herd, were *cattlemen*. It made for some lively discussions at the Red Bull Saloon and the Courtesan House.

It didn't take Joe Coulter long to discover the Courtesan House. Billing itself as a "Sporting House for Gentlemen," its owner, Maggie DeShay, even advertised her services in *The Last Word*:

The Courtesan House
a
Sporting House for Gentlemen
Where
Beautiful and Cultured
Ladies
Will provide you with every
Pleasure

Maggie made no apologies about running a whorehouse. "Why should I be ashamed of it?" she would reply to anyone who questioned her. "I give my girls a clean place to stay and I insist that the gentlemen callers be on their best behavior. If they are not well behaved, I don't let them return."

Maggie had been in town for nearly two years, having come to Epitaph as a member of a theater group. The owner of the repertoire company for which Maggie had worked lost all the box office receipts in an after-show poker game, then tried to take them back at gunpoint. That was a fatal mistake, and he now lay buried out on Boot Hill under a marker that read:

Here lies
LUCIEN THOMPKINS
an actor whose brief hour
upon the stage is no more
his final act ended by
two slugs from a .44

When the rest of the theater company left town, Maggie stayed. She was a beautiful woman, and her role in the theater had inflamed the fantasies of many men. Maggie had only to play upon those fantasies to become a very successful prostitute. It was rumored that she had been the mistress of a Russian prince during his visit to the American West, and because Maggie knew that such rumors fed the fantasies of men who wanted to ''do it with a woman who had done it with a prince,'' she did nothing to dispel the rumors.

When Maggie made enough money, she built the Courtesan House and hired only the most attractive women she could find. She then went into semiretirement, preferring to manage the affairs of her girls over providing her personal services to the customers.

She reserved the right, however, to make an exception to the no-business rule. And when Joe Coulter came into the entry foyer, Maggie was so taken by his big-framed good looks and his easygoing manner that he became one of those exceptions. When it came time to go upstairs she took him herself, rather than introducing him to any of the other girls.

Joe followed her up, unaware that he had been singularly chosen and that all the other girls were looking on in curiosity because of the rarity of the event.

''This is my room,'' Maggie explained, stepping through the door, then turning to invite Joe in. Her voice had a low, husky quality that Joe liked.

The moment Joe was inside the room, Maggie met him with a kiss. She pressed her body hard against his, then opened her mouth hungrily to seek out his tongue. Joe's arms wound around her tightly and he felt the heat of her body transferring itself to his, as she ground her pelvis against his huge erection.

''Oh, my,'' Maggie said, leaning into him, and looking up into his face through eyes smoky with interest. ''Where did that come from?'' She reached down to grab the bulge in the front of his trousers.

''I reckon I brought it in with me,'' Joe answered.

''You brought it in, did you?'' She smiled. ''Then I intend to do what I can to see that you don't take it out.''

Maggie stepped away from him then and began to undress. She kept her unwavering eyes on him as she divested her clothes, item by item, until she was completely naked before him and her body was golden in the soft light of the dim lantern.

Maggie got down on her knees in front of Joe, then looked up at him. Once more, she put her fingers on the bulge in front of Joe's pants, but this time she began opening the buttons. A second later, Joe felt his organ free as she pulled it out.

"I want you to know," Maggie said as she reached up to wrap her hands around it, "that I don't do this for just anyone." Maggie was so close to the head of it that, as she spoke, her warm breath moved across the skin like the most delicate silk. Her tongue came out, serpentlike.

Joe felt his knees weaken, and he had to brace himself for a moment to keep from falling. He put his hands down to her head and gently moved her to him. Her lips opened to take him. As she worked on him with her mouth, his hands moved down to her distended nipples. Gently, he tried to push her away so he could get undressed, but she protested and reached for him.

"No," she said. "Let me do this for you. I want it this way."

Joe rocked back on his heels and shuddered, then put his hands in her hair and held her as he exploded. Finally, long moments after the last tremors were gone, Maggie stood up and pointed toward the bed.

"Now," she said, baiting him. "Come to bed with me and let's see how much of a man you really are."

At that precise moment Joe's brother, Win, was down the street from the Courtesan House, playing poker in the Red Bull Saloon.

"I'll take three," the man in black said. He put his discards on the table, then began coughing. Taking his handkerchief from his inside jacket pocket, he held it over his mouth until the coughing fit passed. Win noticed that the handkerchief was flecked with blood.

The dealer gave the man in black three cards, then looked over at Win.

"And what about you, sir?" the dealer asked. "How many cards?"

"One," Win said.

"Drawing to an inside straight, are you?" the dealer joked, slapping a new card down in front of Win.

Win was actually trying to fill a heart flush, but when he saw that the card was a spade, he folded.

"Well, Doc Masters, it's going to cost you five bucks to see what I've got," one of the players said.

Win glanced quickly at the man in black. None of the players had introduced themselves and not until that moment did he know that he was playing with Doc Masters. He had never met Doc Masters, but he had certainly heard of him.

Doc Masters looked at his cards, thought about it for a moment, then folded with a shrug.

One of the other players, who had bet heavily on this hand and lost, pushed his chair back from the table.

"Boys, I'd better give this game up while I still got enough to buy myself a beer," he said.

Just as he was leaving the game, three men were coming into the saloon. One of them, seeing an open chair, came over to the table and, without being asked, sat down. It was fairly obvious that the new player had been drinking pretty heavily.

"A person with manners would have asked if he could join," Doc said.

"I got as much right here as anyone at this table," the man said. "My family's been here long before the town."

"We know all about you, Ike Kramer," the dealer said, "and how important your papa was. Are you sure you want to play cards?"

"I'm sittin' here, ain't I?"

"You're also drunk. I don't want you comin' back here tomorrow, complainin' because we took advantage of you while you were drunk."

"What's the matter?" Ike snarled. "You afraid to let me play?"

"Let him play," Doc said. "I've been admiring that hat of his. I might just win it tonight."

Ike took off his hat, a low-crowned, black hat sporting a band of silver conchos.

"You ain't gettin' my hat," he said. He pulled a stack of

bills from his pocket and put them on the table in front of him. "On the other hand, after I take all your money, I might just win that fancy vest you're wearin' to go with my hat."

Doc chuckled. "We'll see, Mr. Kramer, we'll see," he said.

By now Win had heard that Ike Kramer was one of the principals in the dispute between the townspeople and the ranchers, so he studied the new player closely. Ike was of medium height and build, with brown hair, clean-shaven, but with a pockmarked face. He also had a broken tooth.

"What are you lookin' at?" Ike snarled when he realized Win had been scrutinizing him.

"I haven't quite figured out what I'm looking at," Win said.

Ike snorted, then played the cards that were dealt him. Win won that hand. He won the next hand as well, and with that hand was now a few dollars ahead.

"You're a pretty lucky fella," Ike said.

"Sometimes it happens," Win said, as he raked in his winnings.

"Yeah, like it happened yesterday. You was lucky then too, wasn't you? I mean, when you killed Mathis and Pearl?"

Win looked at him, but didn't answer.

"I guess you know they were friends of mine," Ike said. "They were good men, both of them. They didn't deserve to be shot down like dogs in the street. Especially by some drifter who just rode into town."

"That's where you're wrong, Kramer," Doc Masters said. "They *did* deserve to be shot down like dogs in the street. They were both sorry bastards and I should have killed them myself, a long time ago. And as far as I'm concerned—as far as most of the town is concerned—it was good riddance."

"I ain't talkin' to you, Doc," Ike said. "I was talkin' to this man. You *are* the one that killed them, aren't you?" he asked Win.

"I'm the one," Win said.

"You see them two fellas standin' over at the bar?" Ike asked.

When Win looked he saw two men, one large and clean-shaven, the other of medium build with a sweeping handlebar moustache. Both were looking toward the table.

"That is Jim and Frank McHenry. They own a ranch right next to my ranch. Charley and Vernon worked for them. They're all broke up over losin' a couple of good hands, like they done."

"I could tell, this morning, just how upset you boys must be over Charley Pearl and Vernon Mathis getting killed. You showed it at their funeral," Win said. "Oh, wait, that's right, there was no funeral, was there?"

"We're plannin' one," Ike said.

"You're a little late. They buried them this morning," Win said. "They were laid out in plain pine boxes then buried on the far side of Boot Hill without even a marker."

"How do you know?"

"Because I was there," Win answered. "And I was the only one, except for the two gravediggers."

"You always go to the buryin' of men you kill?" Ike asked.

Win flashed a cold look at Ike. "When I can," he answered pointedly. "Sometimes I bury them myself."

Ike didn't expect that answer and he blanched, before he recovered what composure he was able to muster in his drunken state. "Just how many men have you killed?"

"As many as I needed to."

"Yeah? Well, that don't scare me none."

"Mr. Kramer, you seem to be working yourself into a state," one of the other players said. "Why don't you stop talking about it now, so we can play a friendly game of cards?"

"He's right," Doc Masters said. "Quit running your mouth, Kramer. Play cards, or get the hell away from my table."

"This ain't your table, Doc. And it sure as hell ain't your fight," Ike said. "It's my fight. Mine and his." He looked pointedly at Win.

Slowly, Win unbuckled his pistol belt and hooked it across the back of Doc's chair.

"It isn't anybody's fight," Win said. "Yesterday I was forced into a situation not of my making, and I wound up killing two men. I don't want to have to kill you too. So why don't you just calm down? As you can see, I'm not armed."

Ike's features twisted into what might have been a grin.

"Well now, taking off your gun like that to keep from fighting might make some folks take you for a coward. You ever thought about that?"

Win looked into Ike's eyes with a glare so intense that, for the moment, Ike could forget who was armed and who wasn't.

"You wouldn't be calling me a coward, now, would you, Kramer?" Win asked. His voice was quiet and his hands were steady, but the look in his eyes was deadly. "Because I don't think I would like that."

Ike, seeing Win's pistol hanging across the back of Doc's chair, suddenly realized that he had the advantage, and he was emboldened by that fact. He chuckled derisively. "So you don't like it? What can you do about it? You ain't even carryin' a gun," he teased.

Win moved so fast then that the others at the table barely saw it. Before Ike knew what was happening, the barrel of his own gun was poking into his nose.

"I don't need to carry a gun as long as fools like you do," Win said easily. "Anytime I want one, I'll just take yours."

Out of the corner of his eye, Win saw Doc draw his own gun, and for a moment he wondered if Doc was drawing against him. Then he saw Doc pointing his gun toward the bar.

"You two gents take your gun belts off and hand them to the bartender, then get on out of here," Doc said to the other players. "I intend to keep this altercation between the two of them."

Nodding his thanks, Win turned his attention back to Ike. By now, a tiny trickle of blood was flowing from Ike's nose as a result of the pressure from the gun barrel.

"Now, I'll ask you again. Did you mean to call me a coward?"

"No," Ike stammered. "No, of course not. I was just sayin' that people who won't fight, well, sometimes other people might not understand."

"Is that so?" Win asked. He brought the gun down to his side and one by one, emptied the chambers of Ike's pistol. Then, when it was empty, he handed it back to him.

Ike put his pistol in his holster, then held his handkerchief to his bloody nose. "I've got better things to do than throw my money away," he said. "I could be down to the Courtesan House with a woman."

"No, I don't think so," Doc said.

"Why not?"

"Because Miss DeShay has let it be known that you aren't welcome there."

"Yeah? Well there ain't no town marshal now, so just who the hell is goin' to keep me from goin' if I want to?"

"I will," Doc said simply.

Ike looked at Doc for a moment, then shrugged. "Well, the girls there aren't the only whores in town." Salvaging what bravado he had remaining, Ike turned and walked out of the saloon, followed by Jim and Frank McHenry.

Shortly after Ike and the McHenrys left, Doc Masters had another coughing fit and, because this one seemed to go on, he excused himself from the table and walked over to the bar.

"Deal me out of this hand," Win said, taking his money from the table.

A couple of saloon patrons had been waiting for the opportunity to get into the game, and they took the empty chairs as soon as Win and Doc left.

Win stepped up to the bar alongside Doc Masters, who was pouring himself a drink. "You all right?" Win asked.

"Yeah, Coulter, I'm fine," Doc replied. He poured Win a drink.

Win was surprised that Doc had called him by name. Neither he nor Joe had given their name since arriving in Epitaph yesterday. They were still wanted men in some areas of the country, so as a general rule they didn't advertise who they were.

"Have we met?" Win asked.

"Back when I was bounty hunting I ran across some dodgers on you and your brother," Doc replied. "The drawings weren't all that good. But you two fit the general description. You'd be Win, I take it?" Doc tossed down his drink.

"Yes," Win answered. " 'You still a bounty hunter?"

"Nope," Doc said. "And if I were, you wouldn't have any worry. As far as I know, you aren't wanted in Arizona Territory. The wanted posters I saw were in Dodge City.''

"Yeah, they would be in Kansas," Win replied. "I reckon
the ones who rode with Quantrill would be wanted in Kansas
a hundred years from now, if anyone is still around.''

"We all have our crosses to bear," Doc said, taking another
drink.

Deep in Doc's eyes Win could see a soul that, for some
reason, was badly scarred. Win had seen such eyes during the
war. Such men, he knew, were the most dangerous of all,
because they didn't care if they lived or died.

"Hey, Doc. Give us a tune, will you?" someone called from
the other end of the bar.

"Yeah, play somethin' on the piano.''

"You can play the piano?" Win asked.

"A little," Doc replied. Shrugging, he walked over to the
old scarred piano and sat down. He began playing "Lorena,"
and all conversation and laughter stopped during the song.

3

IT WAS TEN O'CLOCK AT NIGHT AND IT WAS COLD IN MEM-
phis, Tennessee. Katie Skyles pulled the lap robe around her
and settled back in the seat of the hired cab. On the seat in
front of her the driver, a large black man, flicked his whip
lightly toward the horse. The horse exhaled clouds of vapor
that floated away, white, in the night air.

The horse's hooves clopped hollowly on the cobblestone
pavement of First Street as they passed the dark stores and
businesses of the commercial district of Memphis. Here and
there a yellow square of light shone from the third or fourth
floor of the quiet buildings.

Somewhere in the distance a dog began to bark; his bark
was answered by another, a little closer. A bottle crashed in a
nearby alleyway and a man laughed drunkenly. Katie twisted
around to see how close the laughing man was to the hack,
and the driver chuckled.

"Don' you be worryin' none, sonny. As long as you in my
hack, you under my protection. They ain't nobody goin' to
come outta no alley and bother any of my passengers. I can
promise you that."

Katie smiled. The driver was a big, strong-looking man and
she was fairly certain he could make good his promise of
protection. She also smiled at the fact that her disguise was
working. He didn't realize she was a woman.

A moment later the hack stopped and the driver twisted around in his seat.

"Here's the railroad depot," he said. "I don't know where you're goin', but I'd sure like to go with you. Fact is, I'd like to take me a trip 'bout anywhere. I ain't never been nowhere but right here in Memphis."

"Thank you very much," Katie Skyles said as she paid the driver. Carrying her small bag, she hurried across Poplar Avenue and into the Illinois Central Railroad depot.

Inside the depot a small potbellied stove roared and crackled. The gold light of the fire shone around the cracks and winked through the little vents of the door, and though it put out a small circle of heat immediately around it, it wasn't effectively warming the entire room. Outside it was cold and damp and there was a promise of snow in the air.

Most Memphians would welcome the snow in the belief that it would wipe out the last vestige of the yellow fever with which the city had suffered for the past five years.

Of course, even if the fever did break it would be too late for Katie. It wouldn't bring her parents back. She would still be left with no known relative except the man her mother had married after her father died. Carleton Pembroke had been a foreman in her father's cotton brokerage firm, and Katie's mother married him because she felt inadequate to the task of running the firm alone. Then, six months ago, Katie's mother had also died.

Pembroke had convinced Katie's mother to change her will on her deathbed so that Katie wouldn't come into her inheritance until she was twenty-five or married, whichever occurred first. "In the meantime, I think you should appoint me as her administrator," he told Katie's mother. "That way I can look out for her until she is mature enough to look out for herself."

Recently, Pembroke had been putting pressure on Katie to marry him. That was something she would never do, so taking $200, which was the most cash she could get her hands on, she planned a midnight escape.

Pulling the brim of her hat down and the collar of her coat up, Katie walked over to the ticket window. There were at least a dozen people in the waiting room, and though none of them paid any particular attention to her, she felt as if every eye could see through her disguise. She needn't have worried. The heavy winter clothes did a good job of concealing her true gender.

"Well, lad, and where would you be going this cold night?" the ticket agent asked.

Katie paused. It was funny but not until this moment had she considered where to go. She had thought only of fleeing— she had not thought of where she would go. "Well, I—I don't know," she stammered.

"You have to have something in mind, at least a direction. Which is it? North, south, east, or west?" the ticket agent asked.

"West."

"Where in the West? Texas? California? Arizona Territory?"

"Arizona Territory," Katie answered.

The ticket agent chuckled. "I shoulda known it. You've been readin' the penny awfuls, haven't you? You're goin' west to be a cowboy."

"Yes, that's it," Katie said. "I want to be a cowboy."

The ticket agent began tearing off tickets and stamping them with a rubber stamp. "Can't say as I blame you. If I was young, I might be doin' that myself. Well, sir, you might want to go west, but you're going to have to go south, first. You'll leave this train in Jackson, Mississippi, then you'll catch the Southern Pacific. That'll take you all the way to Arizona."

"How long will it take?"

"Oh, 'bout a week," the ticket agent said. He took Katie's money and handed her a tag for her baggage. "Just have a seat over there, son. We'll call your train in about ten minutes."

"Thank you."

Katie found a seat within the circle of warmth from the stove and had almost dozed off when the windows of the station began to rattle and the very floors of the stationhouse started to shake. The sound of the train was much louder now, not just the whistle, but the rush of steam and the roar of steel rolling on steel. The darkness outside the depot windows was suddenly bathed in a bright light and when Katie looked outside she saw that the threatened snow had materialized. The falling snowflakes glistened like diamonds in the beam of the approaching engine's headlamp.

Ten minutes later, with Katie in a seat most distant from any other occupied seat, the train pulled out of the Memphis depot with a series of jerks and clanks. As the train rolled through the dark city, the conductor came through the cars, turning down the gas lamps so that soon it was as dark inside as out. Katie pulled her coat up around her, made herself as comfortable as possible, and settled in for the long trip.

"What did you say?" Maggie asked, sitting up in bed so quickly that the sheet fell down to her waist, exposing her breasts.

"I said, why don't you let me take you out to get something to eat?" Joe repeated.

"Oh, honey, you don't have to wine and dine me," Maggie replied. She reached under the sheet and grabbed him. "You've already gotten what you want from me."

"Not everything I want," Joe said. "When I find a pretty woman like you, I like to take her out and show her off."

Maggie laughed again. "Honey, I'm a whore. People don't show off whores."

"I do," Joe said. "Besides, I'm hungry."

"Then, why don't you let me have the cook fix you something? I pride myself on keeping a really good kitchen here at the Courtesan House, and Señor Muñoz is a wonderful cook."

Joe got out of bed and walked over to the chair where he had put his clothes. "Get dressed," he said. "We're goin' out."

"Joe," Maggie said, and this time her voice was quiet and apologetic. "Don't you know how it is with women like me? I don't want to embarrass you, but they won't even let me in the Alhambra. You would understand why, if you knew that half the men in there at any given time are regular customers of mine."

"You'll be with me," Joe said, resolutely. "They'll let you in."

Maggie sat in bed for a moment longer, then laughed.

"All right, why the hell not? I'd like to see the expressions on their faces anyway. Besides, if I'm with a big, strong fella like you, who would dare keep me out? So I'll go with you," Maggie said. "But on one condition."

"What is the condition?"

"I want you to leave your gun here."

"Why?"

"Because if you do feel it is necessary to *defend my honor*," she emphasized the words, teasingly, "I don't want any shooting. You can break a nose if you need to, but I don't want anyone killed."

"All right," Joe said, hooking his gun belt over the head of the bed. "If you say so." He chuckled.

"What are you laughing at?"

"Darlin', just so you know, if I wanted to kill someone, I wouldn't really need a gun."

Maggie drew stares when they went into the Alhambra Café several minutes later, but because nobody wanted to confront the big man who was with her, no one made any effort to deny her entry. The waiter came up to their table as Joe was holding the chair for Maggie to be seated.

"Good evening, Carl, how are you?" Maggie asked.

"Please, Miss Maggie," Carl said, looking around nervously. "You mustn't let on that you know me."

"All right," Maggie said, more quietly. "I don't want to cause you any trouble. What do you recommend, tonight?"

"Tonight, *mademoiselle*, I recommend the Tournedos Alhambra," Carl said, once more affecting his cultured accent. "It is a delightful cut of beef, delicately sautéed and served on a bed of marinated artichoke hearts."

"Excellent," Maggie said. "I'll have that."

"I will too," Joe said, taking his own seat now. "But you'd better double my order. Most of the time those foreign-sounding dishes don't have enough food on the plate to suit me."

"Very good," Carl said, retiring to see to their order.

A few moments later the front door opened and a man

stepped inside. He was obviously drunk and almost lost his
balance, but he caught himself on the door frame. The action
caused his hat to fall off and when he picked it up, Joe saw
that it was decorated with a band of silver conchos. He knew
then that this was no ordinary cowboy. A working cowboy
would not be able to keep such a hat for long; during the
frequent lean times, he would surely sell the silver conchos.

"Maggie, you in here?" he called from the door. "Maggie!" he yelled. He put the hat back on his head.

"Oh, no," Maggie said under her breath. She raised the
menu in front of her.

"What?" Joe asked. "Who is that?"

"That's Ike Kramer," Maggie said. "He's nothing but a
troublemaker and I've forbidden him to ever enter the Courtesan House."

"So there you are, Maggie," Ike said, seeing her for the
first time. "I heard you was in here." He started toward her
but tripped over a chair. He prevented himself from falling
only by grabbing onto a diner.

"You are drunk, sir!" the diner said indignantly. "You've
no business on the streets, bothering innocent people."

"What's that?" Ike asked. He pushed his jacket open and
menacingly put his hand over his pistol. "You tellin' me what
to do?"

"Leave him alone, Ike," Maggie said, speaking up then.
"What is it? What do you want?"

"I want to come to your whorehouse," Ike said. "I promise
to behave myself."

"You're not welcome."

"Why ain't I welcome? My brother's always welcome."

"Billy is a well-behaved young man," Maggie said. "You
are not. Now, please leave. You are causing a disturbance in
here."

"Oh, I'm causing a disturbance, am I? Well, Maggie, you
ain't seen nothin' yet. Wait till you see the disturbance I'm
goin' to cause in your whorehouse if you don't—"

Joe stood up then and took a step toward Ike. Ike stopped.
"Who are you?"

"I'm a friend of Miss DeShay's," Joe said. "Why don't you go away like she said?"

For a moment Ike was intimidated by Joe's size and obvious strength; then he noticed that Joe wasn't wearing his gun. Quickly, he drew his own and pointed it at Joe.

"You stay right there, you big son of a bitch," Ike said. Joe stopped and Ike smiled. "I ought to gut-shoot you right now, you bastard, for butting into business that's none of your concern," Ike said.

"Kramer!" a new voice called.

Ike recognized Doc Masters's voice and the mocking smile left his face to be replaced with one of grim determination. He appeared to have sobered up immediately.

"Doc, you wouldn't shoot me in the back, would you?" Ike asked.

"I never could figure out the concern over whether someone was shot in the back or the front," Doc said. "What's the point? You'll be dead either way. Right now I've got a gun pointed toward the back of your head, and if you so much as twitch, I'm going to shoot you where you stand."

There was no gun pointed toward the back of Ike Kramer's head. In fact, Doc wasn't even wearing a gun.

"I . . . I ain't movin', " Ike said nervously.

"Then put your gun back in your holster and get out of here," Doc ordered.

"I'm doin' it, I'm doin' it," Ike said, holstering his pistol. He turned then and started toward Doc. That was when he saw that Doc wasn't armed.

"Why, you son of a bitch, you wasn't pointin' no gun at me!" Ike said. His hand started to dip toward his own pistol, but he never reached it because Joe stepped up to him and laid him out in one punch. Ike went down with his arms flung to either side.

"Thanks for takin' a hand in this, mister," Joe said.

"Call me Doc," Doc said. "Your brother does."

"You know my brother?"

"Win Coulter? Yes. We met over a game of cards. I'm Doc Masters," Doc said.

Like his brother, Joe had heard of Doc Masters. And, like

Doc Masters, many in the restaurant had heard of Joe and Win Coulter. Joe realized then that any anonymity the brothers may have had when they arrived in town was gone now.

"Glad to meet you, Doc," Joe said. "Won't you join Miss DeShay and me for supper?"

"Thanks, but no thanks," Doc said. "I was just walking by when I saw what was going on in here. I'm going to get a bottle of whiskey and have a few drinks before I turn in. And I've never liked to drink on a full stomach," he added cynically. He touched the brim of his hat, then left.

"What are you going to do about him?" Carl asked, pointing to Ike. In his frustration, Carl had lost his carefully nurtured, cultured accent.

"I'll take him outside until he sobers up," Joe said.

Joe picked Ike up and threw him over his shoulder as easily as if he were handling a sack of flour. Ike's hat lay on the floor; Maggie picked it up and placed it on Ike's upturned butt.

"Well, now, I've never seen that fancy silver hat of his look better," one of the restaurant patrons said, and the others laughed at the sight. Several of the customers followed Joe through the door, then watched as Joe dropped Ike into the nearest watering trough.

In one of the rooms of the Courtesan House the air was redolent with the musk of sex. Suzie McGuire lay on the bed and looked over at Billy Kramer. Billy Kramer, still nude, was standing by the window, looking through the curtain down onto Front Street.

"What are you looking at with such interest?" Suzie asked.

"My brother," Billy answered. "He's down there in a watering trough, making a damn fool of himself."

"Your brother is good at that," Suzie reminded him.

"Yeah, I know," Billy said. He took his trousers from the foot of the bed and began pulling them on. "I'd better get him home."

"He's a big boy. Can't he take care of himself?"

"He's my brother," Billy said, as if that explained everything. He finished dressing, then started for the door. He looked back at Suzie and smiled at her. "Besides, it looks like you're going to have a busy night. There must be two dozen gents waiting downstairs."

"I know," Suzie said. "The Lucky Strike Mining Company paid their men a bonus today."

"If I don't get out of here you won't have a chance at any of that bonus money."

"Have I ever rushed you, Billy?" Suzie answered.

"No," Billy agreed. "You haven't."

"Nor will I," Suzie promised. "You can stay as long as you want. You know that."

"Yes," Billy said, and there was an expression in his eyes for a moment that showed that this relationship might be a little deeper than the normal relationship between a prostitute and her customer.

"Billy, I . . ." Suzie started, then she stopped. She knew what she was, and she didn't want to push it.

"Yes?" Billy asked.

"Nothing," Suzie replied. She smiled. "Send the next one up, will you?"

"I'll select someone who is fat and baldheaded," Billy teased as he closed the door behind him.

Suzie lay back on the bed and waited for her next customer. It was going to be a long, hard night.

Epitaph, unlike many of the villages in the Arizona Territory, did not exist prior to the annexation of Arizona to the United States. Founded by Americans, it was much more American in nature than most of the other towns of the Southwest. However, the mines did require a large labor force; therefore, Epitaph did have a Mexican presence in the form of a Mexican *barrio,* on the south side of the railroad tracks.

Here, in the small adobe buildings that housed the Mexican workers and their families, the nights were darker, for only the cantina was well lighted. The other structures were either in total darkness or barely illuminated by burning embers of mesquite wood or fat-soaked rags, because few could afford candles and fewer still kerosene lanterns.

There were no hotels in the *barrio*, and no restaurants except for the food served in the cantina. There was nothing like the Courtesan House either, but there were whores. The Mexican women who engaged in the trade did so from their own houses. In many cases the whores had children who were comfortable with the knowledge that their mother was a *puta*, because they knew of no other existence.

Most of the *putas'* customers were Mexican workers, who couldn't afford the American whores, nor would they have been welcomed by them. However, many of the customers were American, some attracted to the women because of their dusky beauty, others because a Mexican whore cost less than half as much as an American.

One habitué of the Mexican whores was Deputy Sheriff Deekus Taggart. His attraction to them was easily explained. As deputy sheriff, Taggart was able to coerce the Mexican women into providing him with free service. He was also a brutal man who enjoyed hurting and often left the women whimpering in pain when he finished, and the American whores would not put up with that.

Fourteen-year-old Carmelita Gomez sat in the darkened corner of the tiny house she occupied with her two younger brothers and baby sister. A gaily decorated blanket hung from a rope that divided the house into two rooms. On the other side of the blanket, Carmelita could hear the squeaking of the rope-and-wood-frame bed, the gurgling grunts of the *alguacil*, and the barely controlled whimpers of pain of her mother.

She heard a loud smack, and her mother cried out.

"You like that, don't you?" Taggart's voice growled.

"*No, señor,*" Carmelita's mother replied.

There was another smack, louder this time. "Don't lie to me, bitch! I know you like it! All you Mexican whores like it."

"Carmelita," Manuel asked. "Why is Mama crying?" He spoke in a very quiet voice, as they had been trained to do whenever their mother was on the other side of the blanket with a visitor.

"Shh," Carmelita answered, holding her finger across her lips. "Remember, there is no talking now."

Carmelita had a piece of string tied into a circle; she put

her fingers into the string, then began showing her brothers all the tricks she could perform. It kept them so entertained over the next few minutes that they were unaware of the building crescendo of sound behind the blanket, which Carmelita knew signaled the beginning of the end of Taggart's visit.

When she knew it was over, she handed the string to Manuel, suggesting that he try to manipulate it as she had. Manuel's efforts kept him and Pablo occupied, which was what she wanted, because she needed some time on her own.

Moving quietly to the part of the room where the cooking utensils were kept, Carmelita found a butcher knife. Then, before Taggart appeared from the other side of the blanket, she went outside to wait.

A few moments later, Taggart stepped outside.

"*Señor?*" Carmelita called.

"What? Who is there?" Taggart asked.

Carmelita had been in the shadows of the building, but she stepped out now, into the silver splash of moonlight.

"Who are you?" Taggart asked. Then, when he examined her more closely, he recognized her. "Wait a minute, you're her daughter, ain't you?" He pointed toward the house behind him with a jerk of his thumb. "I seen you in there."

"*Sí, señor.* I am Carmelita."

"Well, what do you want, Carmelita?"

"One dollar."

"A dollar? Haw!" Taggart said. "Now, why would I want to give you a dollar?"

"Because I will let you have this," Carmelita said. Quickly, she pulled her dress up over her head, then off, holding the bunched-up cloth in her right hand. She stood before him, totally nude, her young body barely mature, with small breasts and a silky fuzz of emerging pubic hair.

"Oh, shit!" Taggart said.

"You do want me, don't you?" Carmelita asked. With her left hand, she touched herself. "I have heard you tell mama that someday I would be a good *puta.*"

"Well, now, the acorn doesn't fall far from the tree after all, does it?" Taggart asked. "All right, girlie, you want to learn what it's all about, do you? Taggart will show you."

"One dollar?" Carmelita asked.

"A dollar? All right. I don't give any of the other Mex whores a dollar, but I never had me one so young before. You might just be worth it."

Carmelita waited until Taggart stuck his hand into his pocket, then, dropping the bunched-up dress, she lunged at him with the butcher knife.

"What the hell?" Taggart gasped when he saw what she intended. Moving quickly, he stepped to one side, managing to avoid her rush. Then he reached out to grab her knife hand.

Carmelita had lost her only advantage—the element of surprise. Taggart easily took the knife from her hand, then pushed her up against the adobe wall of the house. That moved them into shadows so dark and so deep that someone passing within ten feet of them wouldn't even know they were there. Taggart clamped his left hand over Carmelita's mouth so she couldn't cry out.

"Now, let ole Taggart show you what this is all about," he said.

4

IT WAS EARLY MORNING, AND THOUGH MOST SELF-respecting roosters had announced the fact long ago, half a dozen cocks were still trying to stake a claim on the day. The sun had been up for quite a while but the disk was still hidden by the mountains in the east. The light had already turned from red to white and here and there were signs of Epitaph rising.

A pump creaked as a housewife began pumping water for her morning chores. The first whistle at one of the mines up in the hills called to the miners and somewhere a carpenter had already begun hammering.

Win was awakened by the early-morning sounds, and he poured a basin of water for his shave. He stood by the open window and looked out on the town. He and Joe had been here for nearly a week now, long enough for him to measure the intensity of the disagreement between the people of the town and the ranchers and cowboys of the county.

Under normal circumstances Win believed he would have sided with the cattlemen's position. The cowboys were rugged men who were more at home in the saddle than in a parlor, and Win and Joe related to that.

But the townspeople regarded the Kramers and the Mc-Henrys and the cowboys who worked for them not as rugged individualists but as a bunch of ruffians . . . hell-raisers who had grown wild on the range and were only too anxious to let off steam when they came into town. Often, letting off steam meant shooting their guns, if not at each other in some spontaneous duel, then at any target that might catch their fancy.

Regardless of Win's normal predilection, he had been drawn in on the townspeople's side, first when he killed Mathis and Pearl, and then again when he and Ike had a run-in. He also found it easy to side with the town because Doc Masters, who had become a good friend, was solidly in the camp of the townspeople. And Maggie DeShay, who was perhaps exercising more influence over Joe at the moment than any other citizen of Epitaph, took the position that though there was no absolute right and wrong in the conflict, the town was more right than the cattlemen, especially the Kramers and the McHenrys.

The leading troublemaker of all was Ike Kramer. Win had only seen Ike's brother, Billy, from a distance. Most spoke well of Billy, even the townspeople, and since the younger Kramer had done nothing to cross him, Win had no reason not to believe that he was the well-behaved young man everyone made him out to be.

As Win shaved, a couple of freight wagons rolled slowly through the streets, just beginning what would be a day-long journey to Tucson. The shopkeepers were very busy sweeping the wooden porches and boardwalks clean, the better to attract potential customers. A cowboy who had just awakened from a drunken night on the street was wetting his head in a watering trough.

There was a knock on his door.

"Win? Win, you 'bout ready for some breakfast?" Joe called.

"Yeah," Win said, reaching for his shirt. "I'll be down in a minute."

Joe was waiting on the front porch of the hotel when Win came down. Joe stretched, then took a deep breath. "Beautiful morning, don't you think, Win?"

"I guess so," Win said.

"I like this town," Joe said. "I could stay here a while."

"That's what you said about the last town."

"Yeah, well, I think that's because I always like where I am, better than any other place," Joe said seriously.

Win looked at Joe trying to figure out what he'd said, then he laughed. "Whatever you say, Little Brother," he said.

They started toward the Alhambra Café, passing the general store on the way. A Mexican was picking through the fruits and vegetables the store owner had on display on the front porch of his store.

"Good morning, Señor Muñoz," Joe called, cheerily.

"Good morning, Señor Coulter," the Mexican replied with a polite tip of his hat.

"Damn, Little Brother, do you know everyone in town already?" Win asked.

"Not everyone," Joe replied. "Just the ones who are important. Señor Muñoz cooks for the whores over at the Courtesan House."

Win laughed again. "Whores and cooks," he said. "Not everyone, just the ones who are important."

Win was having a second cup of coffee and Joe was having another batch of pancakes when three men approached the table, all wearing suits. None were wearing guns. Win had been here long enough now to recognize all of them. The short, bald-headed man with chin whiskers but no moustache, was J. C. Malone, editor of the Epitaph newspaper, *The Last Word*. Malone was also the mayor of the town. Emmet Taylor, a very rotund man with a round face and glasses that magnified his eyes, was the banker. Martin Jackson, tall and thin with sunken cheeks, black hair, and dark eyes, owned the hardware store and the funeral parlor.

"Gentlemen, excuse us for disturbing you at your breakfast, but I wonder if we might have a few words with you," Malone said.

"Go right ahead, Mayor," Joe replied. "As long as we don't have to stop eatin'." He carved off a large piece of ham and stuck it in his mouth.

"I was just wondering . . . that is, we were wondering, how long were you planning on staying around our town?"

Win took a swallow of his coffee and studied the mayor and his delegation over the rim of the cup.

"Are you telling us you want us to leave?" he asked, calmly.

"No!" the mayor barked. "Heavens, no, nothing like that. I hope you wouldn't think that."

"You asked how long we were planning to stay—what did you expect us to think?"

"It's just that, well, since Marshal Corbett was killed, we've been a town without law. And no town can afford to be without law."

"I don't know about that," Win replied. "I've always figured that if everyone sort of minded their own business, there'd be no need for law."

"Yes, well, that's the problem. Everyone doesn't mind their own business," Malone said. He looked over at Jackson. "Tell them about your, uh, customer," he said.

"Yes," Jackson replied. "It's a terrible thing. As you gentlemen may know, in addition to owning the hardware store, I am also the town undertaker."

"Yes, I saw you at the cemetery when Mathis and Pearl were buried," Win said.

"This morning, oh, such a tragic case, a young girl was brought to me," Jackson said. "A beautiful young Mexican girl, a child, really, no more than thirteen or fourteen years old."

"The thing about this girl, gentlemen," Malone said, impatient with Jackson's telling of the story, "is that she was murdered. Raped and murdered."

"So you see what we mean about this being a town in need of the law," Taylor said. "Course, that was just some Mexican girl, and I figure the Mexicans will take care of their own. But what if it had been one of our girls? Then what?"

"What about Sheriff Bean? Doesn't his jurisdiction also include Epitaph?"

"I assure you, you will find few in this town who are acolytes of Sheriff Freeman Bean," Taylor answered. "In my opinion, he represents the interests of the county, at the expense of the interests of merchants of the town. He will do nothing about this murder, nor would he do anything about it if it had been an American girl."

"Get to the point, Emmet," Malone said. "Mr. Coulter, I, as the mayor, and these two gentlemen, representing the town council, would like for you to become our town marshal. And we want your brother to act as your deputy."

Surprised by the offer, Win put his coffee cup down and stared pointedly at the three men. "You want *me* to be the marshal?"

"Yes," the mayor said. "Well, both of you, actually."

"Mr. Mayor, before this goes any further, perhaps you should know who we are," Win suggested.

"I know who you are. Doc told me. You're the Coulter brothers," Malone said.

"And you also know that there's paper out on us? We're wanted men."

"Are you wanted in the Arizona Territory?"

Win shook his head. "I don't think so. We haven't been in these parts for long."

"Then it doesn't matter to us whether you're wanted some-place else or not."

"Not to you, perhaps. But it might matter to some of your people. Especially when they find out about our background."

"I know about your background as well, Mr. Coulter. The two of you rode with Quantrill," Taylor said. "I'm from Kansas, and I know better than anyone the evil perpetrated by the men from Missouri. My own brother rode with Jim Lane and was killed during an encounter with the Bushwhackers. If I had seen you—or any of Quantrill's riders—during that time, I would have gladly killed you myself. But the war is over and times have changed. Now I'm the banker in a town that is in desperate need of a lawman. I tell you true, to protect my business interests here, I would make a bargain with the devil himself if I had to."

Win chuckled. "And you consider us the devil?"

"I do indeed, sir, I do indeed. But I make no bones about it," Taylor admitted. "This is rough country out here. Perhaps we need the devil on our side."

"Suppose some of those reward posters on us show up?" Joe asked. "Wouldn't it be a little embarrassing to the town council to have law officers who are wanted men?"

"Why should it be?" Jackson asked. "Who would be in better position to destroy any old reward dodgers than someone in the marshal's office?"

Joe chuckled. "Yeah," he said. "He's got a point, Win. We could do that."

"Now, about the pay," the mayor said. "I'm sure you would be interested in knowing how you would be paid."

"Yeah, if I'm going to take a job, I'd like to know how much I'll make," Win said.

"Fifty dollars a month to each of you. The town will pick up the cost of your rooms at the hotel where you are staying now, and the cost of anything you eat here at the Alhambra."

Win laughed. "I take it you haven't seen Joe eat," he said. "But I have to tell you, even with his appetite, I don't know that it's worth it. I've only been here for a week and I already know there's a showdown coming. Fifty dollars a month doesn't seem to me to be enough money to be caught in the middle of it."

"Yes," Taylor said. He cleared his throat. "That's why we have passed a special gambling tax."

"Gambling tax?"

"From now on, the dealer of every card game in town will withhold ten percent of every pot," Taylor said. "That ten percent will go to your office."

"Ten percent of every hand will go to us? What would Doc think about that?" Win asked.

"The gambling tax was Doc's idea," Malone answered. "It was also his suggestion that we ask you two to take the marshal job. He visited me just before he left."

"Doc left?"

"Yes, but only to go to Tucson. He'll be back in a couple of days. I understand he had some business of some sort," Malone said.

"I wonder what sort of 'business' Doc could have in Tucson?" Jackson mused.

"I don't know," Malone answered. He smiled. "But I sure wouldn't want to be the businessman who is crossing him."

"Tell me, Mayor, just how much money would we make from that gambling tax?" Joe asked.

"Suppose I let Mr. Taylor answer that," Malone said. "He is the banker, after all."

Taylor cleared his throat. "I must tell you that when I figured out just how large your take would be, I was opposed to it. My suggestion was that the money should come directly to the town, and the town could then draw from it to pay you a somewhat better salary. But the council overrode my suggestion, opting to give all the money directly to you."

"How much?" Win asked, repeating his brother's question.

"In my estimation, a minimum of one thousand dollars per month," Taylor said.

Win whistled. "And that's not against the law?" he asked.

"The town council voted for it," Malone said. "That makes it legal."

"One thousand dollars a month!" Joe said. "Damn, Win, I didn't know it was possible to make that much money legally."

"All right, Mr. Mayor, you have yourself a couple of marshals," Win said.

"Good," Malone replied. "Now, when can you start?"

"We've already started," Win replied.

That evening, Joe insisted that Win join him in celebrating their new job by a visit to the Courtesan House, and since Win had not yet availed himself of the Courtesan House's services, he accepted his brother's invitation.

Maggie had Señor Muñoz fix them a couple of steaks, then she broke out a bottle of champagne. After dinner, Maggie called all of her girls into the dining room.

"Ladies," she said, "you already know Joe Coulter. This is his brother, Win. They are now the law in town. Whenever we have any kind of trouble, one of these nice gentlemen will help us. So, I'm going to ask that you be particularly nice to them anytime they call on us. And, as our own way of saying thank you to the law, we will not charge them anything."

"As handsome as these two gents are, who would want to charge them, anyway?" one of the girls asked, and the others laughed.

"Now, I'm going to be, uh, busy with this one for a while,"

she said, sticking her arm through Joe's. "I would very much appreciate it if one of you could find it in your heart to entertain the other one."

"Honey, what I've got to entertain him with isn't found in my heart," one of the girls said, making a ribald joke. She stepped up to him and put her arms around his neck, then leaned into him. "My name is Suzie," she said.

"Shame on you, Suzie," one of the others said. "I thought you were Billy Kramer's girl."

"I'm Billy's girl when he's here," Suzie said. "When he's not here I belong to anyone who wants me. You *do* want me, don't you, honey?" she purred. "I'm determined to make you want me."

Win smiled. "I wouldn't want to say no to a woman who is determined."

Win followed Suzie upstairs and she opened the door to her room, then invited him in with a wave of her hand. They began, at once, to get undressed.

"Oh, you have a spot on your shirt," she said as she took his clothes from him. "Why don't you let me give it to Teresa to take care of? After all," she added with a seductive smile, "you won't be needing it for a while."

"All right," Win agreed. "You can take it to her, but hurry back."

"Don't worry about that, honey, I'll be right back," Suzie promised. She left her room without bothering to cover her nakedness, but this was upstairs at the Courtesan House and men and women alike were frequently seen walking up and down the hallways without clothes. On this level a totally different world existed, with its own set of rules and standards. A man who would be embarrassed at being seen in an undershirt anywhere else could walk nude to the privy up here and think nothing of his nudity.

Win lay on the bed as he waited for Suzie to return. It was a brass bedstead with a cotton-stuffed mattress that sat high on coiled springs. He checked the bed to see if it squeaked, and when it did, he smiled. He remembered asking a whore once why she didn't do something about her squeaking bed, and the whore had responded that it was good for business, that the men who were waiting downstairs, listening to it, became even more eager.

At the time Win believed that the squeaking springs was an original idea, but since then he had learned that nine out of ten whorehouse beds squeaked, and he was sure that they all squeaked for the same reason.

The door opened and Suzie's return interrupted Win's musings. She stood just inside the door and looked across the room at Win, lying on her bed.

"She'll have the spot cleaned out and the shirt ready for you by the time you're finished," Suzie said. When she got closer to Win she drew in a little gasp of breath. "Oh, my, you *are* ready, aren't you," she said, reaching down to grasp that which was standing so tall.

"Yes."

Win looked at her. Her breasts, though small, were firm and well formed, tipped by red nipples that were drawn tight now in her anticipation. His eyes traveled down her body to the small triangle of hair at the junction of her legs.

Win put his hand on her inner thigh, then moved it up. He slid his fingers down through the lips of her sex, feeling the slickness of her desire. She moaned with pleasure and began moving her own hand up and down his shaft, feeling its throbbing heat. For several seconds Win's fingers teased, probed, stroked, and massaged until Suzie was squirming in uncontrollable desire.

"Is it true?" Win asked.

"Is . . . is what true?" Suzie asked through clenched teeth. Her breathing was coming in ragged gasps.

"Are you Billy Kramer's girl?"

"I'm anyone's girl who is with me. I'm yours now," she said. "Does that bother you?"

"Hell, no," Win replied, pulling her naked body down on top of his. "Like you said, you're my girl now."

Win felt her as she guided him into the accommodating damp folds of flesh that hid the center of her womanhood. It was well lubricated with the copious flowing of her sex and when he put his hands on her butt and pulled her toward him, he slipped in easily.

Win wasn't a man who enjoyed being on the bottom, so he rolled her over without breaking contact. Expertly, Suzie raised her legs, then wrapped them around him, pulling him even deeper into her. There was no deep sharing of the soul, no exchanged words of love, for love didn't exist and couldn't exist between them. There was, however, a mutual quest for pleasure, and when they came, they came together.

Suzie McGuire lay beside Win after they finished and looked up at the ceiling. Six, she thought. Win was the sixth man she had been with today, and the night was young.

This one had been good. He had been gentle with her and he had treated her as if he actually cared what she liked, wanted, and felt. So many of the others cared about nothing but their own gratification. They weren't always gentle about it, either. If only more men could be like Billy, or Win Coulter, she would never want for anything else in the world.

Most of the girls who were in the business had stories about why they were here. They were orphans, or they were forced into the trade by evil men, or they had been tricked into it. Suzie had no such story. Suzie was a sensualist. She was a soiled dove because it was exactly what she wanted to be.

Deekus Taggart sat at the desk in the sheriff's office. Bean told him it wasn't necessary for him to stay on duty tonight, but Taggart liked to be in the office at night. It helped him to think.

Taggart poured himself a cup of coffee, then laced the cup liberally with whiskey. He stepped over to the window and looked down the long street toward the downtown part of Epitaph.

He'd learned today that Epitaph had hired new law. Win and Joe Coulter, the two men who had only recently arrived in town, were now the town marshal and deputy marshal.

Win was good, too. Taggart had seen him in action. It wasn't so much the way he killed Vernon Mathis. After all, he and Mathis were both holding a gun on each other and Coulter was the only one smart enough to pull the trigger. Taggart took a drink of his whiskey-laced coffee. Hell, he thought, anyone should have enough sense not to just stand there and let the other fella shoot . . . not when you were holding a gun on each other.

No, it was the other thing, the way Win had drawn his gun and fired—almost in the same action—at Charley Pearl. Pearl was standing at the top of the stairs, holding a shotgun, but he was still killed. Taggart was impressed by that.

He took another swallow of his drink.

The question Taggart was asking himself now was, would the new marshals get involved with the Mexicans? Would Coulter even know about the dead Mex girl? And if he did know about her, would he take the time to try to find out what happened?

Two Mexicans had come into the sheriff's office this morning, holding their sombreros in their hand, reporting that the nude body of a young girl who had been found raped and murdered had been found just outside her own house.

Taggart had stood in the corner of the office while Sheriff Bean was taking their report. He was ready, if they accused him, either to deny it or, if necessary, to shoot his way out. To his relief, however, they stated that they had no idea who could have done such an evil thing.

Taggart remembered then, how dark it had been. No one could have seen what happened, and the girl's mother was still inside. He had gotten away with it.

"Jesus," Sheriff Bean said after the two Mexicans left. "What kind of sorry son of a bitch could do something like that?"

"Are we going to do anything about it?" Taggart had asked.

Bean shook his head. "No, what the hell can we do about it? We don't have anything to do with the Mexicans. Let them work out their own problems. It was probably one of them anyway."

"Yeah," Taggart said. "That's what I figure."

Taggart felt safe after his conversation with Sheriff Bean that morning.

But what about the Coulters? Would they think that because

the murder happened inside the town limits, they should look into it? Surely not. Why would they be any more interested in what went on with the Mexicans than Bean was?

Taggart walked back over to refill his cup.

What if they did? he thought. All right, so what? Nobody knew who it was, and there was no way it could be traced back to him. To hell with it. If they want to look, let them.

Taggart was beginning to feel the whiskey now, and as he felt the warmth of the liquor spreading through his body he allowed himself to think, once more, the unthinkable.

The unthinkable was that, last night, as he plunged the knife into the young girl at the precise moment he was having his orgasm, he had felt a greater sensation of pleasure than he had ever before experienced.

And he knew that he would have to do it again.

5

IT WAS HOT WHEN KATIE ARRIVED IN TUCSON. IT HAD BEEN
less than a week since she'd left the snowy cold of Memphis,
such a sharp contrast in so short a time seemed unreal. She
took her jacket off and tossed it across her shoulder, then
braced herself to walk from the shade provided by the roofed
platform into the bright Arizona sun.

An old Mexican woman was operating some sort of food
stand right across the street from the railroad depot. The old
woman didn't have any teeth and she kept her mouth closed
so that her chin and nose nearly touched. A swarm of flies
buzzed around the steaming kettles, drawn by the pungent aro-
mas of meat and sauces. She worked with quick, deft fingers,
rolling the spicy ingredients into something that looked like
pie crust, then wrapping them in old newspapers before she
handed them to her customers.

Katie was curious about the food, so she walked over to the
old woman.

"What is this you are selling?" she asked.

"Tacos," the old woman said. "Very good. You try."

"How much?"

"Five cents."

Katie took out a nickel and handed it to the old woman,
who quickly put together a taco and handed it back to her.

"Hey, tenderfoot, those things go down a lot better with a
beer," someone called. "Or, don't you have beer back east?"

"Yes, we most assuredly do have beer," Katie said.

"*Yes*," the man mimicked. "*We most assuredly do have beer.*"

Katie was surprised by the bantering tone of the man. She had done nothing to antagonize him. Why was he so belligerent? She glanced over toward the man who was tormenting her and flashed him a look of irritation.

The man was leaning against the front of an adobe building with his arms folded across his chest and one leg bent at the knee so that his foot was against the wall. He appeared to be in his twenties, with a dark handlebar moustache and a cowlick of the same color across his forehead. He was dressed in a red checkered shirt and denim trousers with leather chaps. There were two other men similarly dressed who were standing near him, though they hadn't spoken. They were all wearing guns. This was the first time that Katie had ever seen anyone other than a police officer, wearing a gun.

"I don't like that look on your face, tenderfoot. What are you a-lookin' at?" the man asked, standing up straight and letting his arms fall down loosely to his sides.

"Apparently I am looking at an ill-mannered boor," Katie said. She looked away from him then, satisfied that she had put him in his place and hoping that if she dropped it right here, he would go away and leave her alone.

"What'd you call me, boy?" the man blustered. "A boar? Ain't that a hog? You callin' me a dirty pig?"

"No," Katie said. "That's not what I said."

"The hell it ain't. You insulted me, mister. You called me a pig."

"Please," Katie said, growing a little frightened now. This was getting out of hand. "I don't want any trouble."

"Well, you already got trouble, mister, and plenty of it," the man said. "Nobody calls me a pig and gets away with it."

"Please, I'm sorry if I insulted you," Katie said. She was getting a little frightened now. What had she done? How had she gotten into such a situation? All she did was buy something to eat.

"You packin' a gun, tenderfoot?"

"What? No, no, of course not," Katie answered nervously. "Why would I want to carry a gun?"

"If you're goin' to go roun' callin' folks a pig, you'd best start packin' a gun to back you up. Some folks might not be as nice as I am. I'm goin' to give you a chance to defend yourself. Arnie, give 'im your gun. I'm goin' to shoot the son of a bitch, but I want it to be fair 'n' square."

"What?" Katie asked, gasping for breath. She dropped her taco and put her hand up to her throat. "What are you saying?"

"I'm sayin', mister, that I'm goin' to gut-shoot you right here 'n' leave you for crow bait. But I aim to give you a chance. Give 'im your gun, Arnie."

"Buster, this here boy is just a kid. Leave him alone. Hell, he don't even look like he's shavin' yet. Look at that fuzzy cheek."

"Either give the tenderfoot your gun or use it yourself," Buster said menacingly. "It don't make no never-mind to me. I'd just as soon shoot one of you as the other." He turned to face the man who, a moment earlier, had been his friend. He moved his hand to let it hover just over the handle of his revolver.

Katie couldn't believe what was happening. This fool was bent on killing someone and it didn't seem to make any difference to him who it was. He was ready to shoot his own friend if necessary.

"No, no," Arnie said in a frightened voice. He began unbuckling his pistol belt. "I'll give 'im my gun."

"Son, do you really want to fight this pig? Or would you allow me the pleasure of killing him?" a new voice asked. The voice was low and resonant, and the words, though as dramatic as any words Katie had ever heard, were spoken in such an offhand way that one might think he was passing an innocent remark about the weather.

Katie looked at this new player upon the stage. He was tall and thin, with black hair and black eyes, and, except for a maroon brocaded vest, dressed in black from his wide-brimmed hat to his boots. He was casually lighting a long, thin cheroot, but Katie noticed that he, like the other men, also wore a gun. The bottom of his jacket was pushed behind the gun to allow him unrestricted access.

"On second thought," the man went on just as easily, "calling this son of a bitch a pig does a disservice to all the pigs of the world."

Arnie stopped unbuckling his gun belt and he and the other man moved quickly out of the way. Even the old taco woman moved back. Only Katie, who was new to this country and inexperienced in assessing the raw passions that governed its inhabitants, remained in harm's way.

Buster turned purple with anger, but something inside checked it. Anyone who could so coldly and deliberately utter killing words had to be someone to be reckoned with.

"Mister, I got no quarrel with you," Buster finally said. "My quarrel is with this here fella."

"Seems to me like you just sort of picked a quarrel with him," the man in black said.

"He called me a pig."

"Is that a fact? In that case, I think you should thank him for elevating your status."

"What makes you think I'd want to do a fool thing like that?"

"Because I'll kill you if you don't."

Buster laughed nervously. "You'll kill me? And who the hell are you?"

"John is my Christian name," the man said. "But most folks just call me Doc."

"Doc? What are you? A doctor?" Buster laughed. "A doctor is calling down Buster Billings?"

"Yes. Doc Masters."

The expression on Buster's face froze. What had been mere nervousness suddenly gave way to pure panic. Beads of perspiration popped out on his upper lip. "Doc Masters? You're Doc Masters?"

"At your service," Doc said. He flicked an ash from the end of his cheroot.

Buster put both his hands up in the air, then backed away. "L-look, Doc," he stuttered, "I was just havin' a little fun, here. I wasn't really goin' to shoot 'im or anything."

"Tell the boy thank you for calling you a pig," Doc said.
Buster looked at Katie.

"I-I want to thank you for callin' me a pig," he stammered.

"Do you think he's sincere, boy? Or should I just shoot the
son of a bitch now?" Doc asked Katie.

"No!" Katie said. "No, I'm convinced he is quite sincere.
Really, I am."

"All right," Doc said easily. He nodded his head slightly.
"You and your friends get out of here," he said. "And if I
hear of this boy so much as stubbing his toe, I'm coming after
you."

"Don't worry, Doc, we aren't going to do anything, I
swear," Buster said, and he took one or two hesitant steps,
then he and his two comrades broke into a run.

Despite the close call, or perhaps in relief from its passing,
Katie laughed at the sight, and she was joined in laughter by
the old taco woman.

"Here," the old woman said, making another taco. "You
drop one before."

"Thanks," Katie said. She started to pay again but the old
woman just waved her hand.

"No pay," she said.

Katie turned to her benefactor.

"I want to thank you too," she said. "I really didn't call
him a pig, you know."

"Yeah," Doc said. "Well, I just wish you fellas would wait
until you're dry behind the ears before you come out here."

Doc turned and walked away then, as easily as if he had
done no more than provide directions.

Katie wondered about the kind of place she had come to.
She had been frightened to death, and yet despite the fear she
knew she had never been more alive than at the moment of
her greatest peril.

Katie checked into a hotel, signing the register only as "K.
Skyles."

"That'll be a quarter a night," the clerk said. "Payable in
advance."

Katie gave the clerk a dollar bill and the clerk took a key

from a nail. "You're in room three-twelve. That's the top floor, last room to the rear."

"Thank you," Katie said. "Oh, does that have a bath?"

"I can have a tub and some water brought up," the clerk said.

"Please do," Katie said.

Five minutes later a young Mexican boy arrived at her room carrying a tub on his back. He then made several trips back up, bringing buckets of hot water each time until the tub was filled and steaming. Katie tipped him, then contemplated, with great joy, the bath she was about to have. For almost a week she had bumped along on trains, not relaxing in the luxurious Pullman accommodations, but growing dirtier and more tired in what was called "immigrant class." Never mind that she had lost her identity as a woman during the journey, she had almost been dehumanized. But the thought of a hot bath, clean clothes, a good night's sleep in a real bed, and her rebirth as a woman made all that fall away.

The audience stood in tribute as their thunderous applause filled the auditorium.

"Monsieur, you have captivated us all with your brilliant playing. You are the sensation of the year. Tomorrow we leave for Vienna, then—"

"I'm afraid there will be no Vienna. Tomorrow I leave for the United States."

"The United States? But I don't understand. The world is your oyster, monsieur. Why would you go back to the United States? They are fighting a war there."

"That is why I must go. My father has called me back. My homeland, the South, is under siege by invaders from the North. I have an obligation."

"But no . . . you are beyond petty squabbles now. You are a man of the world, a true cosmopolitan. What care you of a war between bickering neighbors? I beg of you, monsieur, do not return. Your music is a gift from God. You speak of obligation and I agree, you do have an obligation. You have a sacred obligation to share your music with the world."

"I'm sorry, Monsieur Mouchette. I must go back."

• • •

Doc woke up then, and the feelings of the dream were so vivid that he could almost believe that Monsieur Mouchette was there in the room with him. It took a moment for him to realize that he was not in Paris, but in his room over the Dry Gulch Saloon in Tucson.

Doc got out of bed and walked over to the chiffonier, where he poured water from the porcelain pitcher into a basin. Then he erupted into a fit of coughing that left him weak and gasping for breath. When at last the coughing subsided, he poured himself a glass of whiskey, drank it, then washed his face, lathered it, and began to shave.

Why did he dream of Paris? That had been many years ago . . . another lifetime ago, when his name had been on the lips of cultured people throughout Europe, when newspapers had lavished praise on him.

"Is this really all you want out of life?" his father had asked him that morning so long ago. "To be a piano player?"

"Papa, the downstairs dandy in a New Orleans bawdy house is a piano player. I intend to be a concert pianist."

"And that's what you want?"

They were standing on a pillared porch in front of the great columned mansion of River Birch Plantation. His father was giving him a going-away picnic, and neighbors and relatives crowded together on the well-kept lawn. Dozens of house slaves hustled about, serving food and drink to the guests.

"Yes, Papa, it is."

"But to do nothing with your life but make music, whether in a bawdy house or on a concert stage . . . seems like such a waste," his father complained.

"Is it a waste to want to do something to make the world a little more beautiful? When you went to Richmond last year, didn't you bring back two new paintings?"

"Yes, but that's different."

"Why is it different? You bought the paintings because they are a part of the life you have made for us, Papa. I believe man was meant for more than mere survival, and you have raised me to believe that. Thanks to you, I've been surrounded by elegance and beautiful things.''

"It isn't entirely thanks to me. You owe a big thanks to cotton and to the money River Birch Plantation makes.''

"Well, then, consider River Birch. This house is as beautiful as a Greek temple. Why do we live in such a mansion when a simple log cabin would protect us from the elements?''

"There's more to a home than a place to get out of the rain. There's—''

"Beauty?''

"Beauty, yes,'' His father paused for a long moment. "All right, John, I see what you mean.''

"Papa, I want to give some beauty back to the world and I know I can do it with my music. I've gone as far as I can go with the teachers in this country. Franz Liszt is the finest teacher in the world and he has accepted me. I can't pass up an opportunity to study under him.''

His father smiled. "All right, go to Europe. You'll get no further argument from me. Besides, I must confess that I remember my own tour of Europe with great fondness. I wasn't married to your mother then, of course, and the women of Paris . . . Oh, how beautiful they are! And you shall have your pick.'' He held up his glass. "You are right, why should I keep you from that? If a concert pianist is what you want to be, son, then I want you to be the best.''

John Masters did go to Europe to follow his dream. And after he completed his studies with Liszt, the master introduced his star pupil to the European concert stages. But when his honor called him back to defend the South, the thunder of the audiences' applause turned into the crash of artillery. Cheers of adulation became the cries of dying men. The man who had returned from Europe seeing the world for its beauty learned of its ugliness. Surrounded by death, life lost its meaning, and when the war was over, John Frederic Masters, Doctor of Music, found that he could not return to the world he had once known.

"Doc" Masters became a drifter and a gambler. Long, dexterous fingers that were so adept at playing the piano were also good at manipulating cards. And when sore losers challenged his veracity, those same quick hands and nimble fingers proved to be exceptionally good at drawing and shooting a pistol.

Once, John Masters's name was on the lips of cultured people everywhere. Now the name Doc Masters was on the tongues of the society's refuse. Mothers used his name to frighten children into obedience, and young gunsels dreamed of the fame they would win for themselves if only they could outdraw and kill the man called Doc Masters.

Back in Epitaph, over on the Mexican side of town, Deekus Taggart stood in the alley behind the cantina hiding himself in the shadows of the *letrina*. The stench emanating from the toilet was overpowering, but Taggart was so consumed with the malevolent craving that had invaded his soul that he was oblivious to the odor.

Normally, Taggart made his initial contact with the whores in the cantina. In fact, he was so regular in doing so that, unbeknownst to him, the whores had worked out an agreement with each other. They kept a watch at the front door of the cantina and when he was spotted, they would position themselves so that only one would be available to him. They passed this odious duty around among themselves so that no one woman would have to suffer his visits all the time.

It was quite late now, and one had seen him this evening, so the one who had been selected for the duty tonight was beginning to consider the possibility that she might be lucky. Perhaps he wouldn't come at all tonight.

Behind the cantina, in the shadows of the alley, Taggart waited. He had been there for at least two hours, and though the smells no longer bothered him, he was getting tired of standing in one place. Several people had come out to use the *letrina* during the course of the evening, but because there was only one toilet serving both men and women, the women had always come together, one standing watch for the other.

Then, about midnight, Taggart's luck changed. A woman came out of the cantina alone and started toward the toilet. She walked with a weaving, staggering gait, indicating that she was already drunk.

She was ideal for Taggart's purposes. She was alone, and because she was so drunk, if she didn't return to the cantina her absence would probably go unnoticed.

Taggart unbuttoned his trousers. He had never been this hard before. It was going to be wonderful.

6

WHEN KATIE LEFT HER ROOM THE NEXT MORNING THERE WAS no question of mistaking her sex. When she went downstairs to take her breakfast in the hotel dining room, she was wearing her best dress and her hair was clean and perfectly set. She was aware of the appreciative glances of the men who were present and, though she had hidden her sex during the train ride out, she welcomed the attention now as proof of having made the full transition back to womanhood. She was also excited about what lay ahead, for this was, she told herself, the first day of the rest of her life.

In school, Katie had been particularly good at mathematics. She had gone on to study bookkeeping under the tutelage of the bookkeeper at the cotton brokerage, mastering the art. After breakfast, she would start looking for employment; she hoped to use her acquired skills to find a position in a bank or an accounting firm.

One block away from the hotel restaurant where Katie was having her breakfast, Doc Masters was sitting in a straight-backed wooden chair in a doctor's office located on the second floor over a furniture store. The diploma on the wall indicated that Jason Shell, M.D., had graduated from the Ohio School of Medicine in Cincinnati, Ohio. There were other totems of his profession scattered about the office as well: a tall glassed-in apothecary case, an examining table, charts on the wall depicting the human anatomy, and a well-worn leather medicine bag.

Doc Masters, who had come to Tucson specifically to see Dr. Shell, had another coughing fit. He held his handkerchief over his mouth until the seizure passed, then put the handkerchief away and looked at Dr. Shell.

"How often do these coughing seizures come?" Dr. Shell asked.

"The really bad ones come at a rate of about one an hour," Doc answered. "The easier ones come more often."

"Do you suffer from the runs? And vomiting?"

"Yes."

"Sweating at night?"

"Yes."

"How long since you started coughing up sputum?"

"I've been doing it for about six months," Doc answered. "I kept waiting for it to go away but it never did. The blood has only been about a month."

"And the vomiting and the runs?"

"About a month."

"I know you are called *Doc* Masters. Is that just what they call you? Or, are you really a doctor? The reason I ask is, I want to know how best to describe your condition to you."

"I am a doctor," he said. "But not a medical doctor. I am a Ph.D."

"A Ph.D.?" Dr. Shell asked in surprise.

Doc laughed. "It's sort of funny, isn't it? A wasted degree. But then, mine has been a wasted life. However, I believe I will be able to comprehend whatever you have to tell me."

"I'm sure you've guessed it by now. You are suffering from pulmonary phthisis. It is more commonly known as consumption. Some doctors refer to it as tuberculosis because of the tubercles, or fine granules that are found in the lungs."

"Is there anything that can be done for it?" Doc asked. "Anything I can take? I've seen ads in newspapers."

Dr. Shell shook his head. "Quackery, all of it," he replied. "If I had my way, anyone who advertised their snake oil to cure what can't be cured would be horsewhipped and thrown in jail."

"So there is nothing to be done?"

"Well, there are places where you can go," Dr. Shell said. "Consumption asylums. If you go to one and do what they tell you to do, you can prolong your life."

"Prolong it for how long?"

"You have what is called fibrocaseous tuberculosis. Fortunately, it is the slowest-acting form of the disease. With supervised care in an asylum, you could live for another five years."

"And if I choose not to go to an asylum?"

"A year, if you do nothing for yourself, maybe three years if you are careful."

"Thanks," Doc said.

"I could get you a list of asylums."

"No, thanks. I'll take care of myself. I'd rather live three years free . . . hell, I'd rather live one year free, than five in a jail."

"They aren't jails," Dr. Shell said. "Some of them are really quite comfortable."

"No, thank you, no asylum for me. All right, what should I do for myself?"

"Get as much fresh air as you can. Always sleep with a window open, but sleep under a blanket, and wear warm clothing. And of course, no more smoking and no more drinking. That is very important. Also, drink as much milk as you can, eat as much meat as you can."

"I have no appetite for food," Doc said.

"Yes, I know, that is one of the really insidious things about this disease. The very thing that you must do in order to survive is difficult because of the lack of appetite brought on by the illness."

"And if I do all these things you tell me, can you guarantee that it will give me three more years?"

"It may. Of course, there is always the possibility that it won't help at all."

"So what you are saying is, I have from one to three years, no matter what I do?"

"If you do nothing to take care of yourself, you won't last over a year. That, I *can* guarantee you."

Doc was quiet for a moment, then he reached for his jacket.

"All right," he finally said. "Thank you, Doctor."

"Doctor Masters," Shell said as Doc was putting on his jacket. Doc looked at him.

"I have heard of you. I know who you are, and the type of life that you lead. And I know that nothing I have told you today is going to change anything. But I had to tell you."

"I understand."

"There is one more thing that I think you should understand. One of the cruelest aspects of this disease is how infectious it is. You can quite easily give it to the ones you care for the most. Women, for example. If you are ever with a woman . . . even for something as innocent as a kiss, there is a very good chance that you will infect her."

Doc was silent for a moment; then, almost imperceptibly, he nodded.

"I understand," he said.

Back in Epitaph, when word of the rape and murder of the Mexican woman reached them, Win and Joe went down into the *barrio* to have a look around. It was as much for curiosity as anything else, for neither of them had any experience with detective work. They walked back to the toilet where the woman's nude body had been found. She had been discovered this morning lying in a pool of blood; her neck had been cut. By the time Win and Joe arrived, the body had already been taken away, but the blood was still there, providing a veritable feast for hundreds of flies.

Neither Win nor Joe had any idea what they were looking for and the odor from the toilet was terrible, so they stayed for less than a minute. They didn't have to be here to satisfy the town. Mayor Malone had already told them that they needn't bother trying to find out who killed the woman since it was "Mexican business" anyway.

Even the Mexicans were less aroused over this one than they were with the first one. The first one had been a young, innocent girl, albeit the daughter of a *puta*. The second victim was herself a *puta*, and though she had two children, they were already living with the victim's sister, so the death of their mother would make very little impact in their young lives.

The fact that Win and Joe would even bother to come to the scene of a crime in the Mexican part of town was enough of an event that it aroused the curiosity of nearly every resident of the *barrio*. They followed Win and Joe back to the *letrina* and stood around, holding handkerchiefs to their noses, speaking to each other in Spanish, and watching as Win and Joe went through the motions of investigating the crime.

"What do you think, Win?" Joe asked as they crossed the tracks back into the American side of town.

"I think they've got one evil son of a bitch living down there with them," Win replied.

"Ain't that the damn truth?" Joe said. "I know there's no chance we'll ever find out who's doin' it, but if we did, I could save the town the cost of a rope. I'd strangle the son of a bitch with my bare hands."

That evening Win and Joe Coulter attended the show at the Catbird Theater. They were there because the owners of the theater had gone to great expense to bring in a traveling show and they needed some assurance that the rowdy crowds would not break up the show.

The Catbird Theater was so named because of the twelve tiny balcony boxes, called "catbird seats," that surrounded the mezzanine. Inside the boxes, those who paid extra for the privilege could either watch the show or close the curtains and visit with the soiled doves who practiced their avocation there.

Win had put a sign at the door informing all patrons to check their firearms before entering the theater. Before the prohibition imposed by Marshal Coulter, there had been gunplay at the Catbird just about every night. Over a hundred bullet holes decorated the curtains and screens around the stage and perforated the huge seminude portrait of "Fatima, the belly dancer."

Win stood leaning against a post at the rear of the theater, looking out over the boisterous crowd. He didn't mind coming here to keep order. The theater owner was willing to pay Win and Joe $100 each for their time, plus they got to see a show.

Joe had taken a walk around inside the theater and was just now returning.

"How are things looking, Little Brother?" Win asked under his breath. He smiled and tipped his hat to one of the girls he recognized from the Courtesan House. She was hanging onto the arm of a visiting drummer.

"There are some cowboys over there from the Kramer ranch," Joe said. "They're passing a bottle around and talking brave."

"Are they heeled?" Win asked.

"I think they are," Joe said. "None of them are wearing holsters, but I do believe a couple of them have pistols stuck down in their waistbands."

"What do you say we just mosey over there and stand near 'em?" Win suggested. "That way if they start anything, we'll be ready for them."

"All right," Joe agreed.

Suddenly the band played a fanfare and, amid shouts, hoots, and whistles, the theater owner walked out onto the stage. He stood in front of the closed curtains and held his hands up, asking for quiet.

"Ladies and gents," he called.

"There ain't no ladies present!" someone from the audience yelled, and his shout was greeted with guffaws of laughter.

"Oh yeah? Well, what do you call me, you slack-jawed weasel-faced son of a bitch?" a painted woman in one of the catbird seats shouted down.

There was more laughter, but the theater owner finally managed to get them quiet again.

"Lovers of the theater," he said. "Tonight we have an especially thrilling show for you."

The audience applauded and whistled.

"We begin our show with the loveliest burlesque girls to be found anywhere west of the Mississippi. Here they are, the Visions of Art!"

Amid a great deal of whistling and stamping of feet, six beautiful and scantily clad young women began the show. After the girls performed, there was a comedy act between a

moustachioed lecherous old man, and a beautiful, innocent
young girl.

*LECHEROUS OLD MAN: My dear, may I tell you that
you are as lovely as a daisy kissed by the dew?*

*YOUNG GIRL: Why, it wasn't anybody by that name
who kissed me. It was Steve Jones, and I told him I
feared everyone would find out.*

There were a few other jokes like that one, and then a man
billed as "The World's Greatest Magician" made his appearance. He introduced his assistant, a lovely young woman who
looked suspiciously like one of the Visions of Art.

"And now, friends, I shall perform a feat the likes of which
you have never seen before. My lovely assistant will fire this
pistol at me, and I will catch the bullets with my teeth!"

Win had seen the trick before and he knew how it worked.
The magician's assistant fired blanks while the magician
jerked his head back in a bit of ham acting, then spit out slugs
he held concealed in his mouth.

Suddenly, one of the three cowboys from Kramer's ranch
stood up and pointed a revolver toward the stage.

"Catch this one, professor!" he shouted.

Quickly, Joe managed to reach him just in time to deflect
his shot, while the terrified magician and his assistant hurried
from the stage to the guffaws of the audience. One blow from
Joe's big fist knocked the cowboy out, and Joe turned to the
others and held out his hand.

"If any of you gents are carrying a gun, you'd better give
them to me now."

The two remaining cowboys looked at each other for a moment; then, with hangdog looks on their faces, they pulled
pistols from their waistbands and handed them over.

Joe picked up the one he had knocked out and tossed him
over his shoulder.

"I'll let him spend the night in jail," he said. "Maybe his
manners will be better in the morning, when he's sober."

Joe was back to the theater in time to see the concluding

acts. Then, after the curtain came down, most of the audience started down the street for the Red Bull Saloon. Win and Joe stood at the door and watched the theater patrons file out, thankful that the three cowboys from Kramer's ranch had caused them no trouble.

One of the patrons who had enjoyed the show was Kyle Rawlings. When he came out of the theater, he had a few drinks over at the Red Bull with one of the crib whores and thought about availing himself of her services, but decided not to. He and his men had been rounding up unbranded calves for the last two days and tomorrow they were going to brand them and turn them out into the herd. It promised to be a busy day, so reason told him he would be better served by returning to the ranch and going to bed.

The ride back to his ranch took about forty-five minutes, and as soon as he dismounted and started to unsaddle his horse, someone came toward him, moving out of the shadows. It was so dark that Kyle couldn't see the person's face and for a moment he thought the worst. Cautiously, he let his hand slip down to rest on his pistol. Then he recognized his foreman by the physical feature that gave him his nickname, and he relaxed.

"Hello, Slim. I thought you would be in bed by now. You and the other boys left at least an hour before I did," Kyle said as he returned to the job of unsaddling his horse.

"We got a problem, boss."

"What kind of problem?"

"When we got back home, I went out to Yellowslide Canyon to check on the calves we cut out for branding, just to make sure they were all right."

"And?"

"They're gone, boss. Ever' damn one of 'em."

"Damn. How did they get away? Did the fence fall?"

"They didn't get away. Someone took them."

"Rustled?"

"That's what they was, all right," Slim said. "And I know who done it."

"Who?"

Slim had something in his hand, and he held it out to show it to Kyle.

"What's that?" Kyle asked. "It's too dark to see."

"It's a silver concho," Slim said. "Off someone's hat. I found it out there where we were keeping the cattle."

"There's only one person around here who wears silver conchos on his hat," Kyle said.

"Ike Kramer," Slim said, before Kyle could.

"Yes."

"I've got all the men up and dressed," Slim said.

"What for?"

"So we can go after the son of a bitch. Don't forget, boss, those calves belong to us, too."

Kyle put his hand on Slim's shoulder. "Slim, suppose we did go after him. What would we do but start a range war? Remember, we aren't dealing with your average rustler here. We're dealing with another rancher, and a big one at that. If we go over there with a bunch of men, we aren't going to do anything but get a bunch of men killed."

"So, does that mean we don't do anything at all?"

"We can go see Sheriff Bean," Kyle suggested.

"Shit," Slim said, spitting. "What the hell good would that do? Ike Kramer has Sheriff Bean's pecker in his pocket, you know that. And his deputy, Taggart, is such a slimy son of a bitch that I don't see how even Bean can put up with him."

"That may be so," Kyle said. "But like it or not, Bean is our only choice right now."

It was hot the next morning as Ike Kramer took a drink of water from his canteen and watched the cattle being herded into the McHenry holding pen for branding. He laughed as he thought of how easy it had been to take them. They were all penned up just waiting to be taken.

Last night, just as Ike had figured, Kyle and most of his men were in town watching the show. That had made it very easy for them. Billy had also gone in to see the show, and that was important because Billy would not have stood by quietly while Ike, Jim, and Frank took Kyle's calves. That was why they were brought here, to the McHenry ranch, instead of being taken over to the Kramer ranch.

With the traveling show providing the distraction they needed, Ike, Jim, and Frank McHenry simply pulled down the fence that Rawlings had built across the open end of Yellowslide Canyon and moved the calves out. They got away cleanly.

Jim rode over and reached for Ike's canteen. He took a drink, then used the back of his hand to wipe away the water that dribbled down his chin.

"Hell, this is as easy as takin' candy from a baby. They ain't a brand on a one of 'em," Jim said. He laughed. "We'll have 'em all branded in no time. Then Rawlings or anyone else will have bloody hell proving these cows didn't belong to us all along."

"How many did we get?" Ike asked.

"Near as I can make out, about a hundred and ten or so," Jim answered. "And even immature calves is bringin' twelve dollars a head at Tucson, 'n' twenty dollars a head at Kansas City. There's several hundred dollars, just slick as a whistle."

Ike laughed. "And Billy thinks he's the smart one in the family."

Jim took a chew from a plug of tobacco, then offered the plug over to Ike. "You gonna tell your brother?"

"Hell no, I ain't goin' to tell him," Ike answered. "He's so lily-livered, he'd be for givin' the cows back." Ike took a chew from the proffered plug, then handed it back.

"I don't know, Ike," Jim said. "Sometimes I think you cut your brother a little short. I think if it ever come down to it he'd take a stand for you."

"If it ever come down to somethin' like that he wouldn't even be around," Ike growled. "You ever seen the little bastard drunk?" he asked.

"No."

"No, and you ain't a'gonna, either. I tell you, he's just different from the rest of us, that's all."

"Then if your brother ain't goin' to be in on this, we're goin' thirds, not halves," Jim said.

"Thirds? What do you mean?"

"I mean a third for Frank, a third for me, and a third for you. Not half for you, and half for me and Frank. Besides, we're the ones runnin' the risk. We're keepin' the cows here until we sell them."

"Won't be no risk once we get your brand on them," Ike said.

Jim smiled. "That's another thing," he said. "Once we get the McHenry brand on them, if we wanted to, we could claim 'em all an' there wouldn't be nothin' you could do about it. When you look at it like that, we're bein' generous to cut you in for a third."

Ike glared at Jim, then took his hat off and turned it in his hand for a moment while he thought about what Jim had said. He ran his hand along the band of conchos and noticed that one was missing. He wondered where it might be.

"What do you say, Ike? Is it a deal?"

Ike sighed, then put his hat back on. "I guess a third is better than nothin'," he said. "I don't reckon I've got any other choice."

Jim smiled victoriously. "I don't reckon you do," he said. "Come on, we've got some branding to do."

7

"YOU SURE YOU WANT TO GO THROUGH WITH THIS?" SHER-
iff Bean asked as he and Kyle rode up the long road from the
entry gate to the Kramer house. "I mean in these parts callin'
a man a cattle rustler is 'bout the worst thing you can say
about him."

"I haven't called him a cattle rustler yet," Kyle said.
"Right now, I'm just wantin' to see if he might have lost a
silver concho. You might even say I'm doing him a favor.
And, in return for that favor, I'd like to take a ride through
some of his stock. Particularly the branding calves, see if perhaps I can find any of mine."

"I thought you said you hadn't branded them yet."

"I hadn't."

"Then how do you plan to recognize them?" Bean asked.

"There's one or two I might recognize," Kyle replied.

They reached the front of the house, then got down from
their horses and walked up the steps of the front porch. Ike
Kramer met them at the door. He greeted Bean, then saw Kyle.

"What are you doing here, Rawlings?" he asked.

"Mr. Kramer, if you don't mind, I'd like to take a look at
some of your calves."

"My calves? What for? You plannin' on buyin' some?"

"He ain't talkin' buyin', Ike," Bean said. "He says some
of his cows were stolen."

Ike Kramer glared at Kyle for a long moment. "Accusin' us of stealin' ain't very neighborly," he said.

"I'm not accusin' you, Mr. Kramer."

"Then what are you doin' here?"

"Like I said, I'd like to take a look at your brandin' calves."

A horse came around the corner of the house then, and Kyle looked over to see Billy.

"Hi, Kyle," Billy greeted in a friendly voice. He dismounted and started toward him.

"Billy, this here fella has accused us of cattle rustlin'," Ike said.

Billy's eyes flinched, and for just a moment Kyle saw something like sadness in them. The look passed quickly, however, and Billy resumed an expression of unruffled calm.

"You know, Rawlings," he said quietly, using Kyle's last name this time. "There have been folks shot for calling other folks horse and cow thieves."

"I know," Kyle replied. "And there have been people hanged for stealing horses and cows."

"Seems to me like we're at an impasse here," Billy said. "If you're wrong, I ought to shoot you. If you're right, you ought to hang me."

"So far I haven't accused anyone," Kyle said. "Like I told your brother, all I want to do is have a look at your brandin' calves."

"All right," Billy said. "Come on, I'll show you around."

"We ain't got to do that, Billy," Ike said. He looked at the sheriff. "Unless you got a warrant," he added. "You got one of them things, Bean?"

"No."

"Then you got no business messin' around in our business," Ike said.

"Let me show him around, Ike," Billy said. "We don't have anything to hide."

Ike was silent for a moment; then he held his arm out, as if in invitation. "Go ahead, Rawlings," he said. "Take a look around."

Kyle, Billy, and Sheriff Bean remounted, then rode around

the corner of the house out toward the branding pens. There, a hundred or more calves milled about.

"There they are," Billy said when they reached the pens. Kyle dismounted, then climbed up on the fence and started looking out over the calves. Though most calves looked alike, he could remember having noticed three or four with rather distinctive markings during the roundup and he was certain he would be able to recognize them if he saw them now. He stood there for a long moment, staring intently at the small herd.

He saw none that he could identify.

"See any of yours?" Billy asked.

Kyle shook his head. "None I could identify," he admitted. He climbed down from the fence.

"When were these cows supposed to have been stolen?" Billy asked.

"We finished rounding them up yesterday," Kyle said. "We were going to get to the branding today, but my foreman discovered them missing last night."

"What makes you think we took them?" Billy asked.

Kyle looked at Billy. "The truth is, Billy, I wouldn't have believed you had anything to do with it, even if I had found them here," he said. "I figure it was that no-good brother of yours."

Billy squinted his eyes. "Careful, Rawlings. Like you said . . . he *is* my brother. You got any particular reason for accusin' him?"

Kyle pulled the concho from his shirt pocket and showed it to Billy. "We found this out where the cattle were," he said.

At that moment Ike came up to join them. "Found any of your cows, Rawlings?" he asked mockingly.

"No."

"What made you think they would be here?"

"Because he found this where he had been keeping his branding calves," Billy said, holding out the concho Kyle had given him. "The calves are gone."

Ike got down from his horse and went over to take the concho from Billy. He held it up to his hat, laying it over the place where one was obviously missing. "Well, I'll be damned," he said. "So, that's where it was."

"You got any idea on how it wound up on the ground of my empty cattle pen?" Kyle asked.

"Don't have any idea at all," Ike replied. "I prob'ly lost it in town sometime last week."

"You expect me to believe that?" Kyle asked.

Ike stared at Kyle as he put the hat back on with the concho now in place.

"Yeah," he said. "I expect you to believe it."

"Billy?" Kyle said. "Billy, I know you aren't a thief. What do you think about this?"

Billy looked at his brother and, once again, Kyle thought he saw a flash of sadness in his eyes.

"I believe my brother, Rawlings," Billy said.

"Come along, Rawlings," Sheriff Bean said. "There's nothing more for you out here."

"You *are* going to investigate, aren't you?" Kyle asked.

Bean sighed. "Suppose you tell me just what I'm supposed to investigate. You came out here to look at the calves like you wanted. Did you find anything?"

"No."

"Then we're leavin'." The sheriff, who had not dismounted, turned his horse and started to ride away. Frustrated, Kyle stood his ground a moment longer. Then, suddenly, he felt something hard poking him in the back. When he turned around he saw that Ike had pulled his rifle from his saddle scabbard and was pointing it at him.

"Well, if you ain't a'gonna go like the sheriff said, I might just shoot you where you stand," Ike said ominously.

Kyle reached his hand out as fast as the strike of a snake and grabbed the rifle away from Ike as clean as a whistle. Ike let out a bellow of surprise and started for his pistol, but Kyle brought the butt of the rifle up in a vertical stroke, catching Ike under the chin. Ike went down and Kyle whirled and had the rifle leveled toward Billy in almost the same moment, catching Billy with his pistol half out of his holster.

"Leave it, Billy, please!" Kyle shouted.

Billy let the pistol slip back down into his holster.

"I don't want to hurt you, Billy. I figure you got some good in you. But if you keep taking up for your brother, you're going to get yourself killed one day.''

"We all have to die sometime,'' Billy said, easily.

"Yeah, but there are a hell of a lot of things more worth dying for than Ike Kramer.''

Ike sat up then and rubbed his chin.

"Sheriff,'' Ike said, glaring at Kyle. "I want you to get this son of a bitch off my property, now.''

Bean drew his pistol and pointed it at Kyle. "Rawlings, if you don't come along right now, I'm going to lock you up for trespassing,'' he said.

"What are you going to do, Sheriff, shoot me over a trespassing violation?'' Kyle asked.

"If I have to,'' Bean replied. "Come along now. You've looked at the calves and you didn't find any of yours. I've done all I can do for you.''

"Yeah, I'm sure you have,'' Kyle said. Tossing Ike's rifle to the side, he mounted his horse. "Thanks a lot for your help, Sheriff,'' he added sarcastically.

Billy watched as Rawlings and the sheriff rode off, then walked over to his brother. Ike was still sitting on the ground and Billy reached out to give his brother a hand up.

Ike put his right hand in Billy's left, but as Billy was helping him up, he suddenly threw a whistling roundhouse right crashing into Ike's jaw. Ike went down again.

"Hey!'' Ike shouted. He sat up and rubbed his jaw. "What the hell was that all about?''

"Don't you get up again, Ike,'' Billy said menacingly. "If you do, I swear, I'll knock you down again.''

"What's gotten into you?''

"For one thing, I don't like being lied to,'' Billy said. "And for another I don't like being made part of a felony, even if it is to protect my own brother.''

"I don't know what you're talking about,'' Ike said.

Billy stepped up to Ike and hit him again, this time with a backhanded blow that stung, but didn't have any real chance of knocking him out.

"Cut that out!'' Ike called. "What's that for?''

"I told you," Billy said. "I don't like being lied to. Now, where are the calves you stole?"

Ike rubbed his chin again, then sighed. "They're over at the McHenrys'. I was going to cut you in on it, Billy. I was going to make sure you got your share."

Billy walked over to his horse and swung into the saddle.

"What are you going to do?"

"Nothing," Billy said.

Ike sighed. "Good. I thought maybe you were going to do something foolish like run after Rawlings and tell him."

Billy pointed at Ike. "Ike, if you ever do anything like this again, you won't have to worry about someone coming after you."

"Why is that?" Ike asked.

"Because I'll kill you myself," Billy said. He clucked to his horse and rode away.

Ike sat on the ground for a moment longer, watching Billy disappear in the distance. Then he stood up and dusted the dirt away from the seat of his trousers.

Back in Tucson, Katie was discovering that getting a job was going to be a much more difficult task than she had thought it would be. She had tried with accounting and brokerage firms, she had applied for bookkeeping positions with most of the merchants in town, and she had tried in two of Tucson's three banks. She was now sitting in the office of Ed Matthews, president of the Arizona Cattleman's Bank.

"Let me get this straight. You are applying for a position as bank clerk?" Matthews asked.

"Yes."

"I must confess to a degree of curiosity, young lady. What makes you think any woman would be considered for such a position?"

"Not *any* woman. Me. I am good in mathematics and I have been trained in the art of keeping books," Katie replied. "I assure you, sir, I am perfectly qualified to be a bookkeeper, teller, or clerk, or to fill any other position a bank may offer."

"Not in my bank, you aren't," the president said resolutely. Then, seeing the expression on Katie's face, he softened his tone somewhat. "Look, miss, I don't know how it is back east, but out here, if my customers thought there was a woman involved with their money, why, they would withdraw their accounts so fast your head would swim."

"It isn't fair," Katie complained. "I'm as good as any man. I shouldn't be denied the right to make a living just because I am a woman."

"Miss, no one said life was fair," the banker replied. "Listen, do you need a job real bad?"

"Yes, I'm afraid I do. If I don't find employment, I shall soon be desperate," Katie said.

"I have a friend," he said. "You might be just what she is looking for."

"She? A woman? Who is she? Where will I find her?"

The banker held his hand out in a shushing fashion, then walked to the door of his office. He closed it, then came back to his chair.

"As I said, she is a friend of mine," he said, speaking very quietly. "She also banks with me, though her business is in Epitaph."

"Epitaph? What is that?"

"It's a town about twenty miles southeast of here," he said.

"What an unusual name for a town."

"Well, Epitaph is an unusual town," the banker conceded.

"It must be awfully small if it doesn't even have a bank."

"Oh, it has a bank. But Miss DeShay feels that, for business reasons, it is best for her to bank here."

"Miss DeShay? What a beautiful name. What kind of business is she in?"

"She owns a . . . well . . . you might call it a visiting house."

"A visiting house? You mean a hotel? A boardinghouse?"

"Not exactly."

Katie looked confused. "What is it, then?"

"It is a place where men come to, uh, visit women," the banker stammered. "And they pay the women for those visits."

Katie gasped. "You are talking about a bordello! Are you suggesting that I work as a prostitute?"

"No, no! Nothing like that!" the banker said quickly.
"Please, don't misunderstand me, Miss Skyles. You said you
were an accountant. Miss DeShay needs an accountant. And I
assure you, her . . . brothel . . . as you call it, is the nicest place
in Epitaph."

"I don't know," Katie said. "I mean, even if I wasn't expected to be a prostitute, I don't think I could work in such a
place."

"Before you turn it down, I think you should know that
Miss DeShay confided to me that she would pay as much as
one hundred dollars per month for a good bookkeeper. You
are good, aren't you?"

"I'm as good as any man," Katie replied, quickly.

"Then you would be perfect for the job. If you like, I will
write a letter of introduction for you."

Katie ran her hand through her hair as she thought about
the proposition that had just been made to her. One hundred
dollars per month was a fortune. And if this morning was any
indication, the only kind of job she was likely to find in Tucson would be as a laundress or a maid.

"Are such businesses legal here?" Katie asked. "I wouldn't
want to get into trouble with the law."

"It is quite legal," the banker replied.

Why not? Katie thought. Nobody knew her out here. And
if her stepfather ever came looking for her, he would never
think to look for her in such a place.

"All right," she finally said. "If you would, please, write
the letter for me. I shall take the train to Epitaph."

"If you are in a hurry to get there, I would suggest the
stage," the banker said as he began writing the letter. "You've
already missed the train to Epitaph, and there won't be another
until tomorrow." The banker looked at the clock on the wall.
"The stage leaves in just under an hour, and it will get you
there before nightfall tonight."

"Very well," Katie said. "I will take the stage."

The Tucson depot of the Arizona Stage Company was in the
corner of a feed-and-seed store. There were stacks of block
salt immediately inside the door, as well as several sacks of

molasses cake and rolled oats. They filled the room with a sweetly pungent smell.

Harnesses and other trappings hung from pegs on the wall, but in the corner of the building that was used as the stage depot, some effort had been made to separate it from the rest of the store. Here, there was a small counter with a window and a timetable that listed arrivals and departures to such places as Globe, Yuma, Tombstone, and Epitaph.

"I'd like passage to Epitaph, please," she said.

"Yes ma'am, that'll be two dollars," the ticket agent said.

"I'd like one too," a man said, coming up to the window then. When Katie turned she gasped, for it was Doc Masters, the man who had come to her aid yesterday.

"Sure thing, Doc," the ticket agent said. "And to tell the truth, I know that Henry and the new marshal are going to be happy to have you ridin' with them. They're carryin' a money shipment to the Lucky Strike mine."

"The new marshal? Who is the new marshal?"

"That would be me," Win said, smiling, as he came into the depot. "The Lucky Strike asked me to come over here and ride back with their money."

"Win, so you did take the job," Doc said. "Good. I hoped you would."

"It was hard to turn down," Win said. "Especially after I learned about the sweet deal you set up for my brother and me with the gambling tax."

"It's worth a tax if it keeps the games honest, and keeps the trouble down," Doc said.

"I hope everyone else feels that way about it."

"If they don't, they can find a game somewhere else," Doc replied.

"I'd better get out there," Win said, nodding toward the door. "They'll be bringing the money pouch over in a minute or two, then we'll be on our way."

Doc gave a little wave, then walked over to have a seat on a bench but when he saw that Katie was still standing and looking at him, he stood up quickly and took off his hat.

"I beg your pardon for sitting in your presence, ma'am," he said.

"Oh, no, please, sit down, sit down," she said. Quickly, she sat so that he would.

Doc pulled out a cheroot and started to light it, then he hesitated. "Do you mind, ma'am, if I smoke?" he asked.

"Go right ahead," Katie said.

Doc lit his cheroot, then folded his arms across his chest as he waited. Once or twice, Katie caught him looking at her. She knew he was trying to figure out where he had seen her.

"The stage for Epitaph is ready to roll!" someone shouted and, quickly, Doc came over to pick up one of Katie's two suitcases. Henry, the coach driver, got the other. When they went outside to board the stage, Win was already up on the high seat, with a rifle across his lap.

A moment later Henry called to the team, then snapped the whip with a loud report. The horses swung the stage around and began trotting briskly down the main street of the town.

8

KATIE HAD BEEN LOOKING THROUGH THE WINDOW AT THE passing countryside; but, feeling Doc's gaze on her, she looked back at him. Doc was slouched in his seat and he was holding his hands in front of him, making a tent with his fingers. His hands, Katie noticed, were well formed, and his fingers were long and supple.

"Excuse me, miss, but I have the strangest feeling we have met before," he said. "Only I can't remember where and that perplexes me. Surely I would not forget such a lovely lady."

"My name is Katie Skyles. You came to my rescue yesterday," Katie said.

For just a moment Doc looked even more confused; then a glimmer of recognition crossed his face.

"My God! You're the tenderfoot," he said.

"The same," Katie admitted. "The confusion comes from the fact that I had assumed the disguise of a man, thinking it would discourage any unwanted attention."

Doc smiled. "Well, now, that makes me feel a lot better about yesterday."

"Better? I don't understand."

"I've been asking myself ever since it happened, why I butted in. As it was a woman, and not some wet-behind-the-ears tenderfoot who was in danger, I can take comfort in the knowledge that my intrusion was completely justified."

"Not only justified, but most welcome," Katie said. "You

can imagine what a shock it was to just get off the train and stumble into a situation like that. It seems that in affecting my disguise, I was nearly hoist by my own petard.''

Doc laughed. "Indeed," he said. "Nevertheless, I am glad I was able to be of some service. And I will tell you that regardless of what you may have heard about the West, here even the most ill-behaved 'boors,' as I believe you called them yesterday, treat women with respect. You would have been better off by not trying to hide your true gender."

"I believe you are right," Katie replied. "I shall not commit such an error in the future."

"What brings you to Epitaph, Miss Skyles?"

"I'm going to work there, for a Miss Maggie DeShay," Katie explained.

Doc looked at her with an expression of surprise. "You're going to work for Miss DeShay?"

"Yes. Do you know her?"

"I know her. She is a good woman," Doc said. After that, he folded his arms and looked through the window of the coach.

Katie had never met anyone quite like Doc Masters. He was obviously an educated man; his manner of speech indicated that. But there was something else about him. There was a private sadness just beneath the surface. She wondered what private devil plagued Doc Masters.

Up on the box, Win rode silently while the driver worked the horses. Henry had a name for each of his animals, and he insisted to anyone who would listen that they all recognized their own name and responded to his words. He would swear at one of them for slacking, or praise another for doing a good job. Sometimes he teased them, and he created relationships between the horses.

"Princess, look at Gilroy over there. See how he's struttin' his stuff? He's showin' off for you, Princess, what do you think of that? I know, I know, you don't like him, but we all have to work together, so try to get along, will you?"

Henry's conversation with the horses kept him so occupied that Win was left alone with his thoughts. He wondered about the woman down in the coach. Who was she, where was she from, and why was she coming to Epitaph? She obviously wasn't coming for a short visit. He could tell that from the luggage that accompanied her.

Win also thought about the money they were carrying. The pouch contained $20,000. That wasn't quite enough. But if the shipment ever got up to $100,000, he would be tempted to take the money himself. He smiled. Damn, what he and Joe could do with $100,000. They could go to San Francisco. San Francisco was a big town and he was sure there were a lot of beautiful women there. He was reasonably certain, however, that none of them could be any prettier than the girl that was riding down in the coach right now.

Win had to get his mind back on his work. If anyone had a notion to jump the stage, the best place to do it would be at the narrows where the canyon walls squeezed in so tight that there was no room to maneuver. That was just on the other side of the double-back loop they were approaching.

Win waited for the stage to line up with the opening, which would allow him to see anyone who might be waiting for them. There! Just for an instant, he saw them. Road agents were waiting to ambush the stage! The amount of time they were exposed to view was so brief that to any but the most experienced eye, the road agents would have gone completely unnoticed. That was the advantage Win had over many other sheriffs, marshals, and shotgun guards. He had been a road agent himself, so he knew how they thought.

"Henry, they're waitin' for us on the other side," Win said. It was the first time he had spoken.

"You seen 'em for sure?"

"Yep."

"What you want me to do?"

"Just keep on driving," Win said. "I'll get Doc to go with me. We can cut across the top here while you're makin' the loop. With any luck they'll be so occupied with the stage coming that they won't notice us sneakin' up on them."

"I'll pick you up on the other side," Henry said.

Win climbed up onto the top of the stage, then leaned down to look inside. Katie was startled to see his head suddenly appear in her window as he hung upside down like a bat. She gasped.

"Beg pardon, ma'am," Win said. "Doc, you want to come with me?"

Doc nodded.

Win rose back up, took his rifle, and jumped off the stage. Doc opened the door and slipped out with him.

"What's up?" Doc asked. "Someone at the narrows?"

"Yeah, three men," Win said.

Win thought that it was like Doc to know not only why he'd called him, but where the danger would be as well.

Win crouched low as he and Doc ran across the top of the rocks. A moment later they saw the three men. As Win had predicted, they were concentrating so intently on the stage that they didn't suspect a thing.

"Well, well," Doc called out. "Fancy seeing you boys again." They were the same three men who had accosted Katie the day before.

"What the hell? What are you doing here?" Buster yelled. At the same time he yelled, he started firing.

Win and Doc returned fire and it was all over in a matter of seconds. Buster and his two friends lay belly up in the sun.

"Did you have a run-in with those folks yesterday?" Win asked as he casually reloaded his rifle.

"Yeah," Doc said. "They were bothering Miss Skyles."

"Miss Skyles?"

"That's the girl in the coach," Doc said. Like Win, he had reloaded his gun and now he slipped it back into his holster.

"She's a very pretty girl," Win said. "But if you've staked out a claim on her . . ."

"She's going to work for Maggie DeShay," Doc said. "Far as I know, the whole town has a claim on her."

"She's going to work for Maggie?"

"Yes."

Win was surprised. He thought he knew women pretty well. He would never have guessed that the pretty, innocent-looking girl in the coach was a whore.

"These men were foolish to take a chance like this for only

twenty thousand dollars,'' Doc said, nodding toward the bodies.

"My thoughts exactly," Win replied. "Now, if it had been a hundred thousand . . .''

Doc laughed. "Yes, well, Wells Fargo has considered that possibility, I'm afraid. They won't ship that much at one time without one of their own guards.''

In the distance they heard the whistles and shouts of Henry as he worked the team around the tight turn.

"Might as well put the bodies on top of the stage and take them to the next way station. Henry can make arrangements to get them taken back to Tucson for burying,'' Doc suggested.

"If it's all the same to you, Doc, why don't we leave them here for Sheriff Bean to worry about? No need to expose Miss Skyles to the carcasses.''

"Yes,'' Doc said. "I'm ashamed for not thinking of it myself. Let Bean have them.''

Win walked out to the trail and flagged the stage down.

"Any trouble?" Henry asked.

"Nothing that wasn't handled,'' Win answered easily as he climbed back onto the box. Doc got inside and closed the door; then, with a whistle and a shout, the stage was under way again.

They were able to see Epitaph for half an hour before they reached it; they were approaching it through the high country and Epitaph was laid out across a treeless plateau. Seen from this angle, it was almost as if they were flying and Katie could easily imagine herself not in a stagecoach but in a balloon.

"Oh, how lonesome it looks,'' she said aloud.

"I beg your pardon?'' Doc asked. As neither of them had spoken in quite a while, Doc wasn't sure that he had even heard her.

"It seems so lonesome,'' Katie repeated. "For as far as the eye can see there is nothing but emptiness, and yet, in its own fascinating way, it is so very beautiful.''

"Yes,'' Doc said. He quoted a few lines of poetry:

And now 'twas like all instruments,
Now like a lonely flute

"Oh! You know Coleridge!" Katie said, excitedly. She picked up the same poem.

And now it is an angel's song,
That makes the heavens be mute.

"Oh, how wonderful!" Katie said, clapping her hands happily.

"I hope I have not misled you," Doc said. He nodded toward the little town, still visible below. "I'm afraid Epitaph is hardly a testimonial for the human spirit. We kill each other off on a nightly basis."

"Why, whatever do you mean, sir?" Katie asked, puzzled by Doc's statement.

"You are going to have to get used to Epitaph. It's a rather wide-open town, not at all like Tucson."

Katie gasped. "Heavens, you mean it's *worse* than Tucson?" she asked, remembering the encounter with the three men who challenged her the moment she left the train.

"Well, you must remember that Tucson is an old and established city, whereas Epitaph is a new town, built upon silver."

"Is there much silver?"

"More than twenty-five million dollars in the last three years," Doc said.

Katie let out a low whistle.

"Add the rowdy miners to the rambunctious cowboys from the surrounding ranches, mix them with whiskey, gambling, and a few soiled doves, and you can see the source of your trouble."

Katie wondered what he meant by the term *soiled doves,* but she didn't ask.

The sun was just beginning to set by the time the stage entered the town limits and rolled down the main street. Both sides of the street were lined with false-fronted buildings, with the largest being the Red Bull Saloon. There were scores of men wandering up and down the street, many carrying bottles, others staggering and supporting each other to keep from falling. Some, Katie noticed, had already fallen, for there were nearly a dozen or so who were passed out, drunk in the streets.

The stage stopped in front of a three-story building. A big sign in front of the building indicated that this was the Homestead Hotel. There were half a dozen people on the wooden porch of the hotel, and they got up to watch the stage's arrival with interest.

"Here we are, folks," Henry said as he hopped down from the front of the coach. He opened the door and helped Katie down. Win walked around to the back of the stage to take her luggage from the leather boot.

Sheriff Bean arrived just as Henry was passing the money pouch down to Emmet Taylor.

"What is that?" Bean asked, pointing to the pouch.

"Twenty thousand dollars," Taylor said, easily.

"Wait a minute! You had a money shipment and you didn't inform my office?"

"Why should I tell you?" Taylor asked. "For all I know, you'd tell some of your cowboy friends and the next thing I know the money would be gone."

"Are you accusing me of stealin' your money?" Bean asked, angrily.

"Can't very well do that, can I, Sheriff?" Taylor replied. He held up the money pouch. "Seein' as I have the money right here."

Bean blinked his eyes, not sure whether he was being maligned or not. "Yes, well, just remember this. Anytime the coach is outside of the town limits, it's in the jurisdiction of the county sheriff." Making a fist, he pointed to his chest with his thumb. "I'm the county sheriff, which means if anything had happened to it, I would have been responsible."

"You would have been responsible. Yes, that was sort of my idea, as well," Taylor said and Doc laughed. "But you needn't have worried. It was well guarded."

"By who?"

"By Doc Masters and me," Win said.

"How can you guard it? You have no jurisdiction outside the town limits."

"He was acting as Henry's shotgun guard," Taylor said. "That's all the jurisdiction he needs." Taylor looked at Henry. "Did you boys have any trouble?" he asked.

"Nothing we couldn't handle," Henry answered. "Three men tried to hold us up, but Win and Doc left them dead, out on the trail."

"At Cutback Pass?" Taylor asked.

"Yes."

"The dumb bastards always try it there. You'd think by now everyone would know better," Taylor said.

The information that three men had been killed on the trail was a surprise to Katie. No one had mentioned anything about it to her.

"Are you telling me you just left three dead men out on the trail?" Sheriff Bean asked.

"That's county jurisdiction," Win said. "We figured we would leave them for you."

"And just what am *I* supposed to do with them?" Bean sputtered angrily.

"Bring 'em in, or let the buzzards have 'em," Win said. "It makes no difference to me."

"Will you be staying here at the hotel, miss?" Henry asked Katie. "If so, I'll have your luggage carried inside."

"No, she'll be staying with me," Maggie interjected, arriving at that moment.

There was a collective gasp from more than a dozen men when they heard that Katie would be staying with Maggie. The thought of this beautiful young woman being a whore caused half of them to start planning their next visit to the Courtesan House.

"You are Katie Skyles, aren't you?" Maggie asked.

"Yes."

"I thought so. Mr. Matthews telegraphed me that you would be arriving on the stage. But he neglected to say how beautiful you are. You will be working with me. I am Maggie DeShay."

Maggie's greeting was so warm and genuine that she won

Katie over right away. She stuck her hand out and Katie shook it.

"I am pleased to meet you," she said. "But I would be perfectly willing to stay in the hotel. I wouldn't want to put you out."

"Nonsense, you wouldn't be putting me out at all. Besides, you'll find my place much nicer than this, I promise you. And free lodging comes with the job."

"In that case, I will be happy to stay with you," Katie said.

"Dan, do be a dear, would you, and carry Miss Skyles's bags down to the Courtesan House?" Maggie said to one of the men.

"I'd be proud to," Dan answered. He took the two suitcases from Win, then started down the street toward a large white Victorian house. Compared to every other building in town, the house looked like a mansion.

"Oh, my, is that where you live?" Katie asked, pointing toward the house.

"Yes, that's the Courtesan House. Welcome home," Maggie said.

As Katie lay in bed that night, the first night in what was to be her new home, the sounds drifted up from downstairs: the low rumble of men's voices, the soft, seductive replies of the women, interspersed with occasional guffaws of laughter. Through the open window she could hear piano music from the saloon, and, surprisingly, the distant sound of a trumpet. Hollow hoofbeats echoed from a horse being ridden up the street, and out in the desert she heard the mournful wail of a coyote.

Gradually the sounds subsided, and one by one the lights across the town were extinguished until, at last, it lay as a cluster of dark buildings, visible only because of the silver wash of the three-quarter moon.

Lying in her blood-soaked bed on the Mexican side of the town was Maria Sanchez, another murder victim. Unobserved, Deekus Taggart hurried up the dark alley, returning to his own room at the rear of the sheriff's office. Clutched in his left hand was the cross he had taken from the whore's neck. He would put it in a little box he was keeping under the bed in his room. The box already contained the bracelet he took from the woman he had killed behind the cantina and the dress he had taken from Carmelita when he killed her. None of the things he had taken had any real value, but they were important to him. He could take them out and remember the exquisite pleasure they represented. That was good for a little while; but after a while the reminders weren't enough and he would have to go down into the *barrio* and kill again.

9

WHEN KATIE OPENED HER EYES THE NEXT MORNING SHE LAY with her head on the pillow for a moment or two, wondering where she was. A bright splash of sunlight spilled in through the open window, showing wallpaper that featured a repeating design of baskets of blue flowers.

"Mary! Mary, you get those clothes hung up on the line, do you hear me?"

"Yes, Mama," a young girl's voice answered.

The voices came from outside. They drifted into the room on the soft breeze that filled the muslin curtains and lifted them out over the rose-colored carpet.

Katie heard the little girl singing a cheery morning song and when she raised her head to look outside, she discovered that she was looking down onto an alley. The little girl was hanging wash on the line in the backyard of the house just across the alley behind the Courtesan House. Katie sat up, wondering what time it was. From the position of the sun she knew that it must be fairly late in the morning. She didn't normally sleep this late, but she decided she must have been exceptionally tired from the trip the day before. Also, the town, which had been so noisy last night, was very quiet this morning.

Katie dressed, then went out into the hallway. She saw an old Mexican woman folding towels and sheets and stacking them on shelves in a hall closet. She had never seen so many towels before and she wondered how one place could use so many.

A door opened just across the hall from Katie's room and a pretty young woman stepped out. Katie looked at the young woman in some surprise because not only was she pretty, she was also totally naked.

"Teresa, I ran out of towels last night," the naked girl said. She had long, luxuriant black hair and she brushed her hand through it to push the strands back away from her face.

"I'm sorry," Teresa said. "Please excuse." She gave the young woman a handful of towels. The young woman looked at Katie and smiled. "You must be Katie," she said.

"Yes," Katie answered, puzzled at how the girl knew her name.

"I'm Suzie," the girl said. She extended her hand and Katie shook it, trying to act as if there was nothing at all unusual in her shaking hands with a naked woman. Suzie laughed. "Last night after you got in, Maggie told us all about you."

"How many of you are there?"

"Twelve," Suzie said. "Most of 'em sleep all day and don't come out until night. I'd be asleep myself, but I had an all-night visitor."

"A visitor?"

"A customer," Suzie said.

"Suzie? Suzie, I have to get going," a voice called from the room. A man's body followed the voice, stepping out into the hallway. The man was carrying a gun belt draped across his shoulder. He was wearing a hat and boots, but nothing else. "Oh, hello," he said, sticking his hand out. "I'm Marshal Win Coulter. We met on the stage, yesterday."

"Yes, Marshal, I . . . I remember," Katie said, turning her head aside in embarrassment.

"What's with her?" Win asked.

Covering her hand with her mouth, Suzie laughed. "She isn't one of us, Marshal," she said.

"What do you mean?"

"She came to work for Maggie as a bookkeeper. She isn't a soiled dove."

"What? Holy shit!" Win said quickly, dashing back into

the room. "Why doesn't someone tell me these things?"

Suzie's laughter grew louder and when someone else stuck her head out the door to see what was going on, Suzie told her; soon, everyone who was awake was laughing.

"I'm glad I was able to provide you with your morning entertainment," Katie said, piqued by the laughter. She turned quickly and hurried back into her room.

Despite her embarrassment, Katie couldn't get the vision of Win's nude body out of her mind; she was aware of a sudden, unexpected, never-before-experienced heat that suffused her body. The palms of her hands felt sweaty and there was a weakness behind her knees.

A few minutes later Suzie knocked softly, then came into her room.

"Are you still upset?" Suzie asked.

"I'm not upset, I'm just . . ." Katie let the sentence hang uncompleted.

"You're a virgin, aren't you?" Suzie asked.

"Yes, of course I am."

"Then I don't suppose you've seen many naked men."

"I've never seen any man naked, until a moment ago."

"Then you have every right to be embarrassed, and angry with us for laughing at you," Suzie said. "But, if it's any comfort to you, Marshal Coulter was even more embarrassed than you were."

"Good. It serves him right for coming out into the hallway like that."

"I have to tell you now, though—if you're going to live here with us you had better get used to that," Suzie warned. "Up here, on this floor, we live a different life."

"I am beginning to gather as much. You were naked too, and yet you made no effort to cover yourself when he came out," Katie said. Then, as if putting two and two together for the first time, she gasped. "Oh, my, the two of you were . . ."

"Fornicating?" Suzie suggested, somehow managing to make the word sound, if not innocent, at least acceptable.

Katie nodded yes, but she didn't speak.

"But of course we were. That's what we do here, honey," Suzie said. "You're going to have to get used to that as well."

• • •

Joe was in the Alhambra eating breakfast when a shadow fell across his table and he looked up to see a tall, bearded man wearing a badge.

"You Joe Coulter?"

Joe was instantly alert. He had never seen this man before, but the badge he was wearing was stamped U.S. MARSHAL Was he after Joe? Under the table, Joe put his hand on his pistol.

"I'm Joe Coulter," he said.

"I'm Truman Algood, U.S. Marshal," the tall man said. "I looked for your brother this morning, but I couldn't find him. Someone told me you would be having breakfast over here."

Joe eased the pistol out of its holster and waited for the U.S. marshal to make his move.

"You and your brothers are the town marshals of Epitaph, aren't you?"

"Yes."

"I've got a job I would like you to do. Of course, I'd have to swear you in as a deputy U.S. marshal." He reached for one of Joe's biscuits. "Do you mind? I haven't had breakfast."

"No, help yourself," Joe said, relieved that this apparently wasn't what he thought it was going to be. He let his pistol slide back down into its holster, then held up his hand to get the attention of the waiter. "Carl, bring us some more biscuits, would you?" he called. "And maybe another bowl of gravy?"

Truman used the biscuit plate as his own, and he spooned the rest of the gravy over the biscuits. "I'm looking for some mules," he said, as he picked up a fork and started to help himself. "U.S. Army mules. Two of them."

"Do you have any idea where these mules might be?"

"Yeah, I know exactly where they are."

"Well, then there's no problem. Just go get them."

"They're on the Kramer ranch," Truman said.

"The Kramers stole some mules from the army?"

"No, they didn't steal them," Truman said. "Fact is, they bought 'em, fair and proper. But the fella they bought 'em from stole 'em. That means they're still U.S. Army property. The Kramers have to give them back."

Joe chuckled. "From what I know of them, I don't think they're going to want to do that."

"So, you do know them?"

"Yes, I know them," Joe said.

"If I ride out there and ask them to return the mules, will they do it?" Truman asked.

"I doubt it. But if Billy is there, he might talk the others out of killing you."

"That's what I was afraid of. That's why I want to make you and your brother my deputies. I thought maybe the three of us, along with Sheriff Bean, might be able to get the mules back with no trouble."

"Sheriff Bean? He's agreed to go?"

"I haven't asked him yet."

"Don't bother," Joe said. "The Kramers have Bean in their hip pocket." Abruptly, he stood up. "Let's go," he said.

"Go? Go where?"

"Out to the Kramer ranch to get the mules. Isn't that what this is all about?"

"What about your brother?"

"If I know my brother, he's lyin' butt naked in one of the whores' beds over at the Courtesan House right now," Joe answered. "And I never like to disturb him when he's in that condition. We don't need him. Come on, let's go."

It was a good half-hour ride to the Kramer ranch. Joe had never been there before and he had been wanting to see it. This gave him an excuse.

The ranch first came into view when they topped an overlook; they sat on their horses and looked down at the spread. The San Pedro River swept around the ranch, giving it a year-round supply of water and making it the most valuable piece of land in the entire valley.

Even though Joe had found himself in the opposite camp from the Kramers, he felt an immediate affinity for the ranch and could understand why they would fight to protect it. If someone had come up to him at that moment and offered him a choice of the Lucky Strike silver mine or the Kramer ranch, he would have taken the ranch. The silver would eventually be all mined out, but the ranch would go on forever.

"You ready?" Truman asked, interrupting Joe's reverie.

"Ready," Joe replied.

"Let's do it."

Joe took a deep breath, then slapped his legs against the side of his horse to urge him forward. For a moment he wished he had not been so hasty in leaving Win behind.

They passed under a gate that featured a set of polished longhorn steer horns, then rode up to the front of the house. By the time they got there, Ike Kramer was standing on the front porch, cradling a shotgun.

"Mr. Kramer?" Truman said, touching the brim of his hat. He pointed to the shotgun in Kramer's hands. "That doesn't seem very neighborly."

"You're city law, ain't you? City law's got no business out here."

"I'm a United States marshal," Algood said. "For the purposes of this visit, I have deputized Mr. Coulter."

"Whether you deputized him or not, he is still city law. Maybe you don't know it, but us Kramers ain't been gettin' along none too good with the townfolk, especially the town law. So, I'd say your comin' out here ain't bein' too neighborly."

"Mr. Kramer, could we get down and talk for a while?"

"I can hear you just fine, right where you are," Ike said.

"All right, if you say so," Truman replied. "Mr. Kramer, did you come into a pair of mules, recently?"

"I reckon I did. What's it to you?"

"They belong to the U.S. Army, Mr. Kramer. I'm here to take them back."

The shotgun had been broken open at the breech, but now Ike snapped it shut with an ominous click. He didn't raise the barrel, but the threat had been implied, nevertheless.

"You tryin' to tell me I stole them mules?" Ike asked.

"No, sir, not at all," Truman said. "I know that you bought the mules from a man named Henry Patterson."

"Well, I don't understand. If you're admitting I didn't steal 'em, how can they still belong to the army?"

"Because the mules weren't Patterson's to sell," Truman explained.

"Seems to me, then, that this is a matter betwixt the army and Mr. Patterson. Don't see how it affects me."

"It affects you, Mr. Kramer, because you have the mules and they still belong to the army."

"The hell they do. You said yourself I bought them mules. They belong to me now."

"Mr. Kramer, under the law, you are technically guilty of larceny, just as if you had stolen the mules yourself," Truman explained. "You see, you are guilty of receiving stolen goods. I could arrest you, but I won't. The army is willing to offer a deal. No charges will be brought if you'll return the mules."

"I can't see returnin' what was bought and paid for."

"Like I told you, they weren't Patterson's to sell. Consider this, Kramer. Suppose someone went to Tucson and sold some of your cattle, then the man who bought the cattle came out here with the receipt and wanted to cut out a hundred head or so. Would you give him his cattle? He bought the cows, and he has the receipt to prove it."

"I don't give a damn about the receipt. He didn't buy the cows unless he bought them from me," Ike growled.

"Well, Kramer, you have just made my point," Algood said. "The receipt you have with Patterson is no good either. The mules still belong to the army."

Ike stood there, holding the shotgun pointed at Joe and Marshal Algood for a long moment. Finally, with a sigh, he broke open the shotgun and extracted the two shells, then leaned the empty weapon against the front of the house.

"Never let it be said that Ike Kramer wouldn't cooperate with the law," he said. "Tell the truth, I don't know why I bought the worthless critters in the first place. Take the damned things. They ain't done nothin' from the day I brought 'em in but eat, anyway. I'll go to the barn and get 'em and bring 'em to you, and good riddance."

"Coulter," Truman said quietly, after Kramer left.

"Yes?"

"There's someone around the corner of the house." Truman got off his horse and began adjusting the bridle. Then, moving quickly, he pulled his gun, dropped, and rolled toward the corner. He was lying prone with his gun out and pointed toward the person behind the corner, before anyone knew he was about to make his move.

"Come on out from there," Truman called.

Joe looked toward the corner and saw Billy Kramer stepping out from behind the building with his hands up, hesitantly. He was wearing a gun.

"What were you doin' back there, mister?" Truman asked. "Plannin' on shootin' us in the back once we got the mules?"

"No," Billy said. "I was just listening to what was going on, that's all."

"Why didn't you come 'round front?"

"I didn't want to interfere."

"Shuck out of that gun."

"Marshal," Billy said, his face growing red in anger. "Don't make me do that. This is my ranch, these are my men. If you make me drop my gun, it'll make me look bad in front of them."

"I can't worry about that none. Shuck out of that gun."

"Marshal, let him keep his gun," Joe said. "I don't think he means us any harm."

Algood shook his head no. "My motto is, it's better to be safe than sorry," he explained.

"Don't make him do this," Joe said. "No need to bring shame on the man. After all, they didn't steal the mules. They paid good money, thinkin' they was buyin' them."

Truman looked at Joe, then back toward Billy. "All right," he said. "You can keep your gun, mister. But I aim to keep an eye on you."

"Coulter?" Billy said.

"Yeah?"

"Thanks."

Ike Kramer returned then, leading two mules. He handed the ropes to Truman.

"The halters 'n' rope belong to me. I'd be obliged to have 'em back when you're done with 'em."

"I'll see to it, Mr. Kramer, and I appreciate your cooperation,'' Truman said. He clucked at his horse as he and Joe started back down the road.

Ike and Billy stood there for a moment, watching as Joe and the U.S. marshal rode off.

''Why didn't you kill the bastards when you had the chance?'' Ike snorted in disgust.

''You would've liked that, wouldn't you?'' Billy replied.

''Damn right I would have liked it. It would have made a man out of you.''

''They were only doin' their job.''

''Yeah, well, I got a feelin' that the time is comin' when there is goin' to be a showdown between us and them two new town marshals,'' Ike said. ''And they'll just be doin' their job when it happens. I wonder if I'll be able to count on you?''

''I hope it won't ever come to that,'' Billy said. ''But if it does, you'll find me standin' right there beside you.''

ANOTHER MEXICAN WOMAN KILLED
The Fourth This Month
Mexican Community Frightened

Señora Frederica Arino was found murdered in her bed this morning. The method of murder was a knife slash across her throat. Señora Arino is the fourth Mexican woman to be murdered this month, and the other women were killed in the same way.

There are no leads as to who is committing such heinous crimes, although it is believed that the women are being murdered by one of their own people. Señora Arino was a widow whose husband was killed in a mining accident last year. Since that time she has been making a living as a prostitute. Two of the other murder victims were also prostitutes and the other was the daughter of a prostitute. It is not known whether there is any significance to the fact that all four were connected, in some way, to the "world's oldest profession."

Although all the killings have taken place in the Mexican part of town, and all but one of the victims have been Mexican prostitutes, the fact that there is someone among us evil enough to perpetrate such crimes is having a most disquieting effect on the entire community, Mexican and American alike.

10

IN THE HOPES OF IMPROVING RELATIONSHIPS BETWEEN THE citizens of Epitaph and the ranchers and cowhands from the surrounding area, the town of Epitaph decided to sponsor a spring cotillion. In a meeting in the conference room at the Homestead Hotel, the Epitaph Cotillion Delegation, consisting of the town council, the merchants' council, and the Ladies' Civics and Betterment Committee, had a spirited debate as to whether or not to issue an invitation to Ike Kramer and Jim and Frank McHenry.

The Ladies' Civics and Betterment Committee argued against it, insisting that if they showed up there would only be trouble. But the merchants' council reminded them that the entire purpose of the dance was to try to mend fences, and if they didn't let Ike and the McHenrys attend they would accomplish nothing. Reluctantly, the town council agreed and the dance committee voted to extend invitations to both the Kramer and the McHenry ranches.

"What about Maggie DeShay and the ladies who work for her?" Mayor J. C. Malone asked.

Upon hearing the mayor's suggestion, Mrs. Emma Rittenhouse, chairwoman of the Ladies' Civics and Betterment Committee, pulled her considerable frame up from the chair and, sliding her spectacles up her nose, glared at the mayor. "Absolutely not!" Mrs. Rittenhouse snarled. "In the first place, they are not ladies, they are prostitutes, and in the second place

I am shocked that you would even suggest such a thing!''

"Well, I suggested it, Mrs. Rittenhouse, because you can't very well have a dance without women."

"I assure you, sir, there will be women at the dance," Mrs. Rittenhouse said. "Our entire committee will attend, provided you don't make our attendance impossible by bringing in all the dregs of our society."

"I meant young . . . uh . . . *single* women," Malone said, correcting himself quickly. "Most of the ladies of our town are married, whereas most of the young men who will be attending are single. We should provide them with dance partners."

"I will not countenance any activity that supplies whores to the cowboys," Emma said, and the other ladies applauded her.

"All right, then, what about the new girl Maggie has working for her?" Martin Jackson asked. "What is her name?"

"Katie Skyles," Emmet Taylor answered.

"I am shocked that you would even know the name of any woman who works there," Emma said.

"Miss Skyles is not one of Miss DeShay's girls," Taylor said. "She is a bookkeeper only."

"Then that settles it—we will invite Miss Skyles," Mayor Malone said, ending the discussion.

"And now there is the question of our two new lawmen," someone said.

"No, there isn't question. The Coulter brothers will be invited."

"Those men rode with Quantrill during the war. There is no telling how much blood is on their hands. How could we possibly invite them to the social event of the year?"

"We have pinned badges on those men and asked them to put their lives on the line for us," Mayor Malone said in spirited defense. "This is not even a matter for debate. They *will* be invited . . . and that is the end of it."

At the same time the dance committee was meeting to discuss whom to include, and more important, whom to exclude from their invitation list, Joe Coulter was in the marshal's office, just down the street from the Homestead Hotel. He was play-ing a game of solitaire at the desk when Kyle Rawlings came in.

"Marshal, can I talk to you?" Kyle asked.

"Actually, I'm the deputy, not the marshal, but go ahead," Joe said. Joe needed a red seven, and, peeking into the deck, found one. He played it on the black eight.

"Can you get a card out of the deck like that?" Kyle asked, momentarily distracted by Joe's cheating.

"Why the hell not? I'm playing myself," Joe answered, easily.

"I guess you have a point."

"If you're here about your calves, there's nothing we can do about them," Joe said.

"You know about the calves?"

"Everybody knows about them," Joe said. He turned up an ace.

"Then you know they were stolen."

"Yep. And I know Bean took you out to the Kramer ranch to look for them. You didn't find anything, did you?"

"No. They weren't there," Kyle said. "But I just found out they never were there. They're over at the McHenry place."

"How do you know?"

"One of Slim's pards rides for the Double Nickel spread. He was over at the McHenry ranch last week and saw a pen full of unbranded calves. He had seen ours after we got them rounded up, and he's sure he recognized some of them. The McHenrys stole my cows."

"I wouldn't be surprised," Joe said as he continued to play cards.

"Well?" Kyle said in an exasperated voice.

"Well, what?"

"Well, I want you to go after them," Kyle said. "I told you, they're my cows. I want them back."

Win had come into the conversation in time to overhear enough of it to know what it was about. He answered for Joe.

"We can't go get those calves for you, Rawlings," he said.

"Why the hell not? They're my calves. I'll admit that the McHenrys probably have their brands on them by now, but they're my calves. And everyone who works on my ranch will testify to that fact.''

"I'm not disputing that they're your calves," Win said. "I'm just telling you we've got no authority to go get them back for you, that's all.''

"You're wearin' badges, ain't you?''

Win chuckled and looked down at the star that was pinned to his shirt.

"Yeah," he answered. "Who would've ever thought that the Coulters would be wearing badges? But as far as your cows are concerned, these are worthless pieces of tin. We're the law only from the backside of the Jingle Bell Corral to the other side of Seth Martin's outhouse. Go one foot beyond either one and commit a crime and all we can do is watch you do it.''

"Yeah, well, that ain't the way I heard it," Kyle said, bitterly. He pointed to Joe. "I heard you went out to the Kramer ranch and brought back a couple of mules for the army.''

"Word does get around here, doesn't it?" Joe asked.

"Well, did you go out there for a couple of mules, or not?''

"Yes, I did.''

"All right, so tell me, Deputy Coulter, how is it that you can bring back mules for the army, but you can't help me recover my calves?''

"Because I was deputized, that day, by a U.S. marshal to go with him to get the mules," Joe said. "But it was only a temporary thing. I'm not a deputy U.S. marshal anymore.''

"Then you're telling me there's nothing I can do about it?''

"There's nothing legal that you can do," Joe replied.

"What do you mean, nothing legal?''

"They're your calves, aren't they?" Joe said. "Hell, if they were mine, I'd ride out there and get them back.''

"Are you tellin' me to break the law?" Rawlings asked.

"Why the hell not?" Joe replied, easily, as he looked for a black nine by rifling through the deck. "It's not our law.''

The Epitaph Spring Cotillion took place in the ballroom of the Homestead Hotel. It was held on a Saturday night and from late afternoon on, ranchers and their wives and cowboys and

their girls began arriving in town. Many came into town in
wagons and buckboards carrying their entire families.

For the most part the ranchers were at their best. With their
wives and children along, none of the ranchers were anxious
for any trouble, and the cowboys, aware that their jobs might
depend upon their own good behavior, also managed to put
their best foot forward. The townspeople put their hostility
toward the ranchers aside for the duration of the ball, and some
of them even managed to smile and wave at the wagons and
buckboards as they arrived.

By dusk the excitement that had been steadily building
around the ballroom of the Homestead Hotel was full blown.
The musicians could be heard practicing, and children were
gathered around the glowing windows to peek inside. The ballroom floor had been cleared of tables and chairs and the band
was installed on the platform at the front of the room.

Even though not everyone was there, the band reached a
point of such fine tuning that they were no longer able to hold
back. They plunged into their first song, ''Buffalo Gals.'' After that came ''Little Joe the Wrangler'' and then ''The Gandy
Dancers' Ball.''

By now, horses and buggies were beginning to pile up on
the street in front of the hotel. Every hitching post was full
and the large lot at the Jingle Bell Corral was crammed with
buckboards and wagons. Men and women were streaming
along the boardwalks headed for the hotel—the women in col-
orful gingham, the men in clean blue denims. Many of them
sported brightly decorated vests as well.

There was one other invited guest who required some discussion by the dance committee before they issued her invitation. Although neither Maggie nor any of the girls who
worked for her would be welcome at the dance, the dance
committee decided that Katie Skyles could attend. By now
everyone knew that though she was employed by the Courtesan House, she wasn't one of the soiled doves. And, as she
was an unmarried and very pretty young woman, they knew
that her presence would be an attraction to single young men.

When Katie began questioning the other girls about what
one should wear to such dances, and what they were like, she

learned that there had never been one prior to this one, so there was no precedent. She was also surprised to discover that they had not received invitations.

"I don't understand," she said. "None of you received an invitation? But why not? Why, it's the only subject of conversation in town right now. Surely the invitations have merely been misplaced. I can't believe that you were not invited."

"Katie, think about it," Suzie said. "The wives and daughters of the townfolk will be there tonight. Even the kids. We wouldn't be welcome."

"But, that's awful," Katie protested. "Don't people even give you a chance? Don't they take the time to know you, to see how nice all of you really are?"

Suzie laughed. "Katie, didn't you say you came from Memphis?"

"Yes."

"Did you know any of our kind in Memphis?"

"By 'our kind,' you mean soiled doves?"

"Yes. Did you know any?"

"No."

"I didn't think so. Now, back in Memphis, if you were at a party for your family and friends and several prostitutes suddenly made an appearance, would you have accepted them with open arms?"

Katie looked at Suzie for a moment, then she smiled, sheepishly.

"No," she was forced to admit. "I'm afraid I would not have. I'm sorry."

"Don't apologize, honey. That's just the way things are. We know it, and we don't hold it against anyone, not even the ladies of this town."

"All right. If none of you can go, then I won't go either," Katie said. "After all, I am one of you. I may not be a soiled dove, but I feel that you are all my friends, my sisters."

"Please, you must go," Suzie insisted.

"No, I wouldn't hear of it."

"But don't you understand? If you go, then it's as if a little piece of us is going as well. You must go and look at everything and remember everything so that when you come back, you can tell us all about it.''

Katie looked at Maggie, and Maggie smiled. ''They're quite serious, Katie,'' she said. ''We do want you to go, for all of us.''

The dance had already started by the time Katie left the Courtesan House for the walk to the Homestead Hotel. She could hear the high skirling of the fiddle almost as soon as she was on the street. Under the music was the sound of laughter and the shuffling of feet, and the lilting voice of the dance caller.

Win Coulter was standing at the front door, and when Katie arrived, and he tipped his hat.

''Good evening, Miss Skyles,'' he said.

''Good evening, Marshal.'' Katie had seen him many times since the incident in the upstairs hallway of the Courtesan House, and though the picture had burned itself so indelibly in her brain that she could never forget it, she was able to suppress it whenever she saw him. Even now, though, she felt her cheeks pinken slightly, and again a warmth seemed to flow through her veins.

''Perhaps you will do me the honor of a dance later this evening?''

What would she do? She couldn't turn him down without being rude. And yet, could she be with him without thinking of that moment? Strangely, she heard herself answering, even as she was contemplating the invitation.

''Yes, I would be pleased to,'' Katie replied.

The light and sound that had spilled through the doors were but a tiny bit of the brightly swirling excitement going on inside. Here and there, bright pinpoints of light flashed from beneath an ear, or in the hollow of the neck as a diamond or ruby or emerald caught the golden light from the many candles and kerosene lanterns that were scattered about.

''Grab your partners 'n' form your squares!'' the caller shouted.

The men started toward the young women. For just a moment Katie thought she would be left out—then she saw Win, smiling broadly, coming toward her. He claimed her, and they moved into one of the squares.

The music began with the fiddles loud and clear, the guitars carrying the rhythm, and the accordion providing the counterpoint. The caller began to shout. He laughed and clapped his hands and stomped his feet and danced around on the platform in compliance with his own calls, bowing and whirling as if he had a girl and was in one of the squares himself. The dancers moved and swirled to the caller's commands.

Around the dance floor sat those who were without partners, looking on wistfully, and those who were too old, holding back those who were too young. At the punch bowl table, cowboys added so much of their own alcoholic ingredients to the punch that though many drank from the bowl, the contents never seemed to diminish.

The dance finished and Katie fanned herself and smiled at Win. Her face was covered with a patina of perspiration and a curl of hair stuck to her forehead. She blew a stream of air across her face and the lock of hair was dislodged.

A couple of the cowboys got into an argument over the attentions of one of the girls and they were glaring and growling at each other, though cooler heads prevailed and the argument was settled without Win taking a hand in it.

"I saw your brother," Katie said. "He was in the kitchen over at the Courtesan House. I think Señor Muñoz was cooking something special for him, tonight."

"Joe isn't much for dancing," Win answered. "But he does like to eat."

A shy young cowboy asked Katie to dance then, and she obliged him. She danced with three others, then again with Win, then with a young miner, then again with Win.

Win, she noticed, had not danced with any of the other women, though Katie saw several of them looking toward him with open invitation in their eyes. The fact that he did dance with her, and was there for her between her dances, gave her a sense of proprietorship that she rather enjoyed.

One of the men she danced with was Billy Kramer, though she felt a little guilty dancing with him because she knew that Suzie liked him.

"I'm only dancing with you as Suzie's surrogate," Katie told him.

"As her what?" Billy asked.

Katie laughed. "That means I'm standing in for Suzie, since she isn't here to dance with you herself."

"Hmm, just how far will you take this 'standing in' for Suzie?" Billy asked.

Katie smiled and pretended that she didn't understand what Billy meant, but in fact she did know, because she knew that Billy was one of Suzie's most regular customers.

A few dances after she had been with Billy, Ike Kramer came over to her. As she was standing with Win Coulter, Ike spoke to him first.

"Good evenin', Marshal Coulter," he said. He pulled his jacket open to show that he wasn't armed. "As you can see I'm not wearin' a gun. What do you say me and you call a truce for tonight?"

"All right by me."

"I promised my brother, Billy, I would be on my best behavior, and I aim to keep that promise."

"Good. Then we shouldn't have any trouble tonight, should we?"

Ike looked at Katie. "I seen you dancin' with my brother a while ago, Miss Skyles. And I'm figurin', why would you settle for Billy when you could have me? How about a dance?"

Katie looked toward Win with an expression of alarm on her face.

Ike, misunderstanding her look, added, "That is, if the marshal don't mind."

"Miss Skyles is her own person," Win said. "She doesn't need my permission. On the other hand, she doesn't have to dance with you if she doesn't want to," he added, pointedly.

That was what Katie wanted to hear, for the truth was she had no wish whatsoever to dance with Ike Kramer. She had heard too much about him from Maggie and the other girls at the Courtesan House, and none of what she had heard was good.

"Thank you for the invitation," Katie said. "But I think I'll pass."

"Why not? You danced with Billy. Ain't I good enough for you? Or, bein' as you work over at the whorehouse, maybe you only dance with them that visit the whorehouse on a regular basis."

"Miss Skyles doesn't need a reason why she doesn't want to dance with you, Kramer," Win said. "She said no, and that's it. Now, move on."

Ike glared at the two of them with such intensity that it frightened Katie, and she took an involuntary step toward Win.

"Miss Skyles, would you care to get a breath of fresh air?" Win invited.

"Yes," Katie answered. "Yes, I would like that very much. Thank you."

It was cooler outside and half a dozen other couples were also taking advantage of the night air.

"Oh, could we take a walk?" Katie asked.

"All right," Win agreed.

They walked the entire length of the boardwalk until they reached the edge of town, then continued on for another hundred yards or so until the sound and the lights of the town were behind them. Now the music from the dance was barely audible. They heard a woman's scream, not of fear obviously, for it was followed immediately by her laughter, which carried clearly above everything.

Ahead of them lay the Dragoon Mountains, great slabs of black and silver in the soft wash of moonlight.

"Oh, look at that," Katie said. "I had no idea that anything this wild and rugged could be so beautiful."

"It is pretty, all right," Win agreed.

"Marshal . . ."

"Why don't you call me Win? To tell the truth, I'm still not quite used to being a lawman. And I sure don't like being reminded of it every time a pretty woman opens her mouth."

"All right, Win," Katie said with a smile. "But Maggie says that you and your brother are good lawmen."

"How good can we be?" Win answered. "Down in the Mexican part of town someone is murdering women and we don't have the slightest idea who it could be.''

"Yes, isn't that awful?" Katie said. "All the girls have been talking about it. They are frightened because the Mexican women are also prostitutes. That's why they like for Joe to be there.''

Win chuckled. "I knew there was some reason Joe spent so much time down there.''

"Maggie really likes your brother," Katie said. "And you know what I think she likes most? I think she likes the fact that nothing can ever come of it. She says that you and your brother are like the tumbleweed. You live on the wind . . . you are only here for a brief time, then you will move on.''

"So Maggie has my brother and me all figured out, does she? What else does she say?''

"She says that you rode with Quantrill. Did you?''

"Yes, we did.''

"What a magnificent adventure that must have been!" Katie said in awe. "I remember my father saying that Quantrill was a true champion of the South and that anyone who rode with him was a hero.''

"There are those who would disagree with you," Win said. "Some would say that we used the Confederate flag as the authority to plunder and murder.''

"But, that's not true, is it?''

"I can't deny it out of hand," Win said. "Truth is, I'm not all that proud of everything I've done in my life," Win said, quietly. He touched the star that was pinned to his shirt. "Even this," he added. "I'm a lawman in name only. I don't have the slightest idea of how to go about being a marshal. I should be looking for whoever is killing those women, but I confess that I don't even know where to start. Kyle Rawlings, who is a good man even though he is a rancher, came to Joe and me for help, and there was nothing we could do for him. There's a big showdown coming between the townspeople and the ranchers . . . or at least the Kramers and the McHenrys, and there's nothing Joe and I can do to stop it.''

"Who is in the wrong?" Katie asked.

"What do you mean?''

"The ill will that exists between the town and the ranchers.

Someone is right, and someone is wrong. Who is in the wrong?''

Win laughed. ''It's easy to see that you're new out here,'' he said. ''You always assume that someone is right and someone is wrong.''

''Why shouldn't I make such an assumption? It certainly makes it easier to solve the problem. All you have to do is go to the person who is in the wrong, and make it right.''

''You think it's that simple, huh?'' Win asked. ''Well, I wish that were so. But in this case there's enough wrong to go around for everyone. However, if all things were added up, I would guess that most of the wrong would belong to the Kramers and the McHenrys. They're the ones who seem to be keeping everything stirred up. And, if you want my opinion, it's because they're trying to cover up the fact that they're throwing a long rope.''

''Throwing a long rope? What does that mean?''

''It means they're doing a little rustling,'' Win said. ''There's no doubt in my mind that Kyle Rawlings is right when he says they stole his cattle. In addition, the Kramers and the McHenrys are just downright mean.''

Katie shook her head. ''No, that's not true,'' she said. ''At least, not for Billy Kramer. He isn't at all like the others. He has always been the perfect gentleman around me, and Maggie and Suzie think he is very nice.''

''Don't be too taken in by him,'' Win suggested.

''Why? Do you know something about him that I don't know?''

''No, but I have known men like him. They seem like nice, quiet men, but they're the kind who can be the most dangerous.''

''But he really is different from his brother,'' Katie insisted. ''I haven't heard anyone say one good thing about Ike, but everyone talks about Billy's good qualities.''

''Just remember this. One of the strongest 'good' qualities is loyalty,'' Win said. ''Everybody admires loyalty. But absolute loyalty blinds you to everything else. If Ike brings things to a head, you can bet that Billy will be right there with him. He may not want to, but in the end his loyalty to his brother will be so strong that he can't do anything else."

"Oh," Katie said, as if getting an insight at that moment. "I understand what you are talking about, now. That's how it was with you and Quantrill, wasn't it?"

"What do you mean?"

"You said you weren't all that proud of everything you did . . . but you did it anyway. It was because of your loyalty to him."

"Yes," Win admitted. "That's pretty smart of you," he added. "I hadn't thought about it like that before, but that's exactly the way it was."

"You *had* thought about it," Katie said. "That's why you know so much about Billy's situation. You just hadn't applied it to yourself before, that's all."

They stopped walking then, and Katie looked back toward the town, now a glowing cluster of buildings on the desert floor.

"Look how far we've come. I had no idea," she said.

"Yeah, I guess we'd better start back, unless we want to wind up wandering, like Moses in the desert," Win suggested.

"I suppose you are right," Katie agreed. "But it's so beautiful out here I feel as if I could stay forever."

11

FROM THE OPPOSITE END OF TOWN, UNNOTICED BY WIN AND KATIE, Deekus Taggart rode in, his horse moving at a brisk trot. He tied the horse off just in front of the hotel, then went in. Standing just inside the door for a moment, he saw Ike Kramer and Jim and Frank McHenry leaning against the wall behind the punch table, all of whom were holding a glass of the drink which, by now, was a concoction that only the most determined drinker could stomach. He started over toward them.

"Hey, Deputy," a cowboy called out from near the punch bowl. "Where you been? You've damn near missed all the fun. You're 'bout a day late and a dollar short for all the doin's."

Taggart looked at the man who called out to him, but he didn't say anything. Instead, he went directly to the other side of the room, where he sought out Ike, Jim, and Frank.

"Hello, Taggart. Get a drink and join us," Ike suggested.

"No time for that. I've got somethin' I think you fellas are going to want to hear," Deekus said.

"What's that?" Frank asked.

Taggart shook his head. "Uh-uh. I ain't givin' this away for free."

Billy was dancing with the daughter of the blacksmith when he saw Ike and the McHenrys leave the dance with Deputy

Taggart. He didn't know where they were going, but figured it was just as well. When Katie Skyles had refused to dance with Ike a few minutes ago, his brother had come back over to stand alongside the wall to brood and drink. That was a dangerous combination for Ike, and Billy had been waiting for the trouble to start.

He was very glad they left, because Billy especially didn't want any trouble tonight. All he wanted to do tonight was have a good time, and to that end, he had his evening all laid out. He would finish this dance, then go over to the Alhambra for supper. After supper, he planned to wind up over at the Courtesan House, where he would spend the night with Suzie.

About five miles out of town, half a dozen men were riding through the darkness, their way lighted by an exceptionally bright moon. Kyle Rawlings was at the head of the group and when the road crested a hill, he stopped and held up his hand. The others stopped with him.

"There it is, boys," Kyle said, pointing to the dark buildings: house, barn, bunkhouse, and granary that lay in a cluster in the little valley below. "The McHenry place."

"Where you think they're a-keepin' our cattle?" Parker asked.

"Mike said he seen 'em over in the feeder pens," Slim said. "That's the feeder pens, over there behind the barn."

"All right, boys, what do you say we ease on down there, real quiet," Kyle said. "Everyone keep together, and keep your eyes open." Kyle urged his horse on down the hill and the others followed. One of the horses whinnied, and its rider leaned forward to pat the animal reassuringly on its neck.

When Ike saw Kyle and his men moving like shadows through the sage, he jacked a shell into the chamber of his rifle and waited.

"Do you see 'em?" Jim McHenry whispered.

"Yeah, I see 'em. They're comin', just like Taggart said they would," Ike said. "Look over there, just this side of that big cottonwood tree," Ike said, pointing.

"Let 'em come. We're ready for 'em," Frank said. He also jacked a round into his rifle.

Ike, Jim, and Frank had come up with ten dollars apiece to buy the information that Taggart had to sell them. For thirty dollars, Taggart told them that he had learned Kyle Rawlings and his men were planning a raid on the McHenry ranch. Ike and the McHenrys left the dance immediately and began preparing to meet them. Ike, Jim, Frank, and eight of the McHenrys' most trusted riders were in positions around the feeder pens, hiding behind rocks, buildings, and other convenient places of cover and concealment. Kyle Rawlings was riding into an ambush.

"There don't seem to be no one around," Slim said. His voice carried well in the darkness, and Ike and the others could hear every word.

"Well, if we're goin' to get our cows back, this has to be the best time for it," Kyle said. "I figure the McHenrys and most of their outfit has to be in town for the dance."

"Yeah, I would be there too, if it wasn't for this," Parker said.

"Which would you rather do, dance or get our cows back?" Leroy asked.

"Seein' as how some o' them cows is mine, I reckon I'd rather be here, a-gettin' 'em back," Parker answered.

As they rode slowly down the hill, they could hear a gentle lowing from the area of the feeder pens. There they could also see the massed shadows of milling cattle. Their cattle.

"There they are," Kyle said, pointing to the feeder pens. "That's about twelve hundred dollars of our money, boys. Let's go get it back."

"*Now!*" Ike suddenly shouted, his voice cutting through the night like a peal of doom. He stood up, raised his rifle to his shoulder, and fired, and with a surprised grunt of pain, Leroy fell from his saddle.

"What the hell!" Slim shouted. "Where did that come from?"

Frightened and surprised by the sudden and unexpected ambush, Rawlings's men tried to control their bolting horses.

"They were waitin' on us!" Kyle shouted, managing to snap off a shot toward the flashes of rifles and pistols that were now shooting at him. "Get out of here, boys!" Out of the corner of his eye he saw another of his men going down.

"Boss, they got Leroy and Parker!" Slim shouted. Getting his horse under control, he jerked it around and dug his spurs into the animal's flanks. Just as he did so, a bullet crashed into the back of Slim's head.

"Slim!" Kyle shouted, but his next word was cut off as a bullet entered his own back, tore through his heart, then exited through his chest.

For no more than half a minute, the night was lit with the muzzle flashes of those who had waited in ambush. The guns roared and bullets whined, then, as suddenly as it had begun, the firefight was over. Now the final gunshot was rolling back as an echo as Ike, Jim, Frank, and the others stood up, cautiously. Not one of the approaching riders was still horsed. Not one of the ambushers had been hit.

Holding smoking guns at the ready, Ike and the McHenrys walked slowly through the dark to look through the twisted forms lying on the ground. None were moving and all were silent. Frank was the first one to them, and he began poking at them with the toe of his boot.

"Any of 'em alive?" Jim called.

Frank looked back at his brother and shook his head. "Don't think so. Ain't none of 'em breathin'."

"Whooee!" Ike shouted. "We got 'em! We got ever' damn one of 'em!"

"What do we do with 'em now?" Jim asked.

"Sometime before mornin' we'll load 'em in a wagon and take 'em into town," Ike suggested.

"And do what with 'em?"

"We'll just leave 'em there."

"When the townspeople wake up and find 'em there, that's goin' to cause quite a stink," Frank said. Then, realizing the double entendre of his comment, he laughed. "Hey, you fellas get that? These here dead bodies is goin' to cause a stink?" He laughed again.

"You think it's a good idea to take 'em into town?" Jim asked.

"Why not? We got nothin' to hide. They the ones come out here to attack us. We didn't go after them. The deputy can vouch for that."

"Ike's right," Frank said. "We got nothin' to hide. And the way I look at it, this'll be a pretty good sign for anyone else that takes a notion to steal any of our cattle."

"Yeah," Ike said. "Or even for somebody who might decide to steal back any of the cattle we already stole."

The three men laughed again and the McHenry hands, who were still up by the feeder pens, were struck by the macabre scene of their employers laughing loudly while poking through the bodies of six dead men.

No one in Epitaph knew about the short, fierce battle that had just taken place out at the McHenry ranch. Here, the laughter and the friendly exchange of conversation continued as the partygoers left the hotel to start back home . . . townspeople, miners, and ranchers alike. The members of the Epitaph Cotillion Delegation were congratulating each other on the success of the event, not only for its social significance, but also because it seemed to draw the townspeople, miners, and ranchers closer together.

They weren't entirely blind to the fact that the Kramers and the McHenrys had left the party early, thus eliminating the biggest potential source of trouble. Still, they told each other, it had been a successful experiment, and should be tried again.

Win offered to walk Katie back to the Courtesan House and she accepted. Then, with good-byes, good-natured shouts, and laughter still ringing in their ears, they started down the street.

"I had a wonderful time tonight, Win," Katie said. She put her arm through his.

"I did too," Win replied.

"I just wish the rest of Maggie's girls could have gone."

"It wouldn't have bothered me any," Win said. "Hell, I don't think it would've bothered anyone except a few of the old crones who don't have anything better to do."

"I know," Katie said. She sighed. "And, sad to say, I was once one of those old crones."

Win laughed.

"What is it?"

"Well, you're not old, and you are anything but a crone," he said.

"Maybe not, but I must confess that my social mores have changed considerably since coming out West. I have seen, and done, and accepted things that I never would have done before. I mean, here I am letting a man I've only known for a short time walk me back to my room in a bawdy house." Katie laughed. "Who knows what I am liable to do next?"

"Yeah," Win said, smiling at her. "Who knows?"

At that moment they heard boots clumping on the wooden sidewalk as someone was chasing after them. Turning toward the sound, Win saw that it was one of the men he played poker with on a regular basis, a man who worked as a freight-wagon driver for the Lucky Strike.

"Marshal Coulter, you'd better come quick!"

"What is it, Tim?"

"That Mex fella, the one that works over to the whore-house? He's in trouble. I'm afraid he's goin' to be killed."

"What?" Katie asked in alarm. "Win, is he talking about Señor Muñoz?"

"Muñoz, yeah, that's the one," Tim said. "Some drunk cowboy is givin' him a hard time."

"We've got to help him," Katie said, starting toward the Red Bull.

"Not we . . . me. You go on home," Win ordered. "I'll take care of it."

The Red Bull was strangely quiet when Win stepped through the door. The piano music, the card playing, and even the conversation had all stopped. Everyone in the saloon had moved to one side of the room or the other, while in the middle stood the Mexican cook from the Courtesan House. Muñoz had an expression of terror on his face, brought on by the fact that a cowboy was pointing a gun at him.

Win recognized the cowboy as a man named Blanchard.

Blanchard had never given him any trouble before, but he was obviously looking for trouble now.

"Muñoz, what is it? What's going on?" Win asked.

"Ask the gringo," Muñoz answered. "I think maybe he wants to kill me."

"Blanchard, what are you doing with that gun?" Win asked. "You know we put a ban against carrying guns tonight because of the dance."

"I didn't have it when I was at the dance."

"The ban was for all night, whether you were at the dance or not."

"That's a mighty dumb idea if you ask me," Blanchard said.

"Well, that's the point, Blanchard. I don't recall asking you about it when I came up with the plan," Win said. He looked around the saloon. "Anyone else in here armed?"

"Nobody else is heeled, Marshal," Sam, the bartender, said. "Ever'one is clean as a whistle."

Win looked back at Blanchard, then held out his hand. "Then that means you're the only one here carrying a gun, and you're the only one here causing trouble. Why don't you give it to me?"

Blanchard shook his head. "Uh-uh. Not until I kill this here Mexican."

"You aiming to kill him in cold blood?"

"Why not? That's how he killed the women."

"What?" Win asked. "Blanchard, what the hell are you talking about?"

"I figured it out," Blanchard said. "You know all them Mex women that's been gettin' killed?" He waved his pistol toward Muñoz. "This is the son of a bitch that's been doin' it."

"What makes you think that?"

"I figured it out," Blanchard said. "I mean, you would too, if you would just stop and think about it."

"All right," Win said. "Explain it to me."

"All them Mex women that's been gettin' killed is whores, right? And this here Mexican works in a whorehouse, right?"

"He works at the Courtesan House," Win said. "Not a Mexican whorehouse."

"Hold on, hold on," Blanchard slurred, drunkenly. "I'm gettin' to that. See, the point is, lots of Americans goes down into the *barrio* to visit the Mexican whores cause they're cheaper. And ole Muñoz here, knows that. So, he figures, if ever'one goes down to see the Mexican whores, pretty soon won't be anyone comin' to the Courtesan House. And if there ain't nobody comin' to the Courtesan House, they won't be needin' no cook and Muñoz will lose his job. So, he decided he'd go down and start killing 'em all off."

"You figured that all out by yourself, did you?" Win asked.

"Yeah," Blanchard answered with a broad, proud grin. "Pretty smart, huh?"

"Damn smart," Win said. He started toward Blanchard with his hand extended. "Let me shake your hand."

Still grinning, drunkenly, Blanchard switched his gun from his right hand to his left, then extended his hand. In a quick, abrupt maneuver, Win managed to snatch the gun from Blanchard with his left hand while at the same time clipping him hard on the chin with his right. Blanchard went down and out.

"You got that bucket of mop water behind the bar?" Win asked the bartender.

"Yeah, I got it."

"Hand it to me."

Sam bent down, picked up the bucket, and gave it to Win. Win poured it on Blanchard, who sat up, coughing and spitting dirty water.

"Muñoz, get on back to the Courtesan House," Win said.

"Sí, señor. Gracias."

"Hey, you're lettin' him go!" Blanchard complained. "I told you, he's the one been killing' them Mex whores."

"Yeah? Well, I can't be bothered with that," Win said. "Come on. I'm throwin' your ass in jail, but I'm not carryin' you down there. You're goin' to have to walk."

Defiantly, Blanchard put his wet hat back on. "What if I tell you I ain't goin' to walk?"

"I'll shoot you in the foot."

"No you won't. You're wearin' a badge."

"Don't let the badge fool you. I'm not like any lawman you ever knew."

"Is that a fact? Well, I'm sittin' right here, 'cause I'm bettin' you won't shoot me in the foot," Blanchard said with a snide smile. Pulling his knees up in front of him, he wrapped his arms around his legs and glared defiantly at Win.

Suddenly, and unexpectedly, there was the loud explosion of a gunshot. When the billowing smoke drifted away, the surprised patrons saw Win standing there, holding a smoking pistol. Win had shot at Blanchard's foot, clipping the edge of the boot sole. The bullet also creased Blanchard's little toe and he grabbed it, howling with pain.

"I guess you lose the bet," Win said. "Now, get up while you can still walk, or I'll fix it so you'll have to be carried. Either way, you're going to spend the night in jail."

"No, no," Blanchard said. "Don't shoot again. I'm goin', I'm goin'." He hopped up as quickly as he could under the circumstances, then, limping, started toward the jail, followed by the laughter of all who were in the saloon.

Over in his room behind the sheriff's office, Deputy Sheriff Deekus Taggart pulled the box out from beneath his bed and looked at it. He touched the dress that Carmelita had held bunched in her hand. He stroked the bracelets the second and fourth women had worn, and he clutched the cross of the third. Then, to those four totems he added a fifth, a string of colored beads.

Out in the *barrio* the nude body of the woman who had last worn these beads lay on the dirt floor beside the crib of her newborn baby.

When the woman's body was discovered by her sister the next morning, word flashed through the Mexican community that *El Bestia* had struck again.

"In the daytime, El Bestia *can appear in any guise he wishes: a bird, a dog, or a lizard,"* the myth said. *"But in the nighttime he becomes half man and half animal: a creature with a horned human head and human torso, but a goat's body from the waist down, complete with male genitalia, furry legs, and cloven hooves."*

12

WHEN KATIE RETURNED HOME TO THE COURTESAN HOUSE she was met in the parlor by half a dozen of the girls.

"She's back!"

"Tell us all about it!"

"Yes, do tell. Was the music just wonderful? We could hear it, even down here!"

They were as excited as schoolgirls as they crowded around Katie to listen to her report of the biggest social event in Epitaph's history.

Noticeably absent were Maggie and Suzie, and, though Katie didn't ask about them, one of the girls volunteered the information that Suzie was upstairs with Billy Kramer, while Maggie was in her room with Joe Coulter.

Katie had danced with Billy earlier tonight, and she found the fact that she had danced with him and now he was upstairs in bed with Suzie to be somewhat erotic. Funny, she thought, how she saw eroticism in so many things now. Even something as innocent as walking out into the desert with Win Coulter had caused her to feel an unexpected heat.

"Well?" one of the girls asked, impatiently.

":Well, what?" Katie replied, putting thoughts of eroticism out of her mind.

"Are you going to tell us about the dance? Or are you going to make us wait until Maggie, Suzie, and the others are here?" one of the girls asked.

"No, I won't make you wait," Katie replied with a little laugh. "I'll tell you everything I can. And if I have to begin again when someone new comes, then what is the harm? But where do I start? What do you want to know?"

"What did everyone wear?" someone asked.

"Yes, were the dresses beautiful?"

"Did the women wear jewelry?"

"Were there good things to eat?"

"Was the music as good as it sounded?"

Katie laughed. "Wait a minute, hold it, one question at a time, please," she said. "Just be patient, I'll tell you everything, I promise."

For the next several minutes Katie did all she could do to make the party happen for them. And whenever one of the girls who had been absent when she started talking drifted into the parlor, she would start over. There was never the slightest complaint from those who had already heard the first part of the story about having to listen again.

Katie's audience seemed insatiable, and she described the dresses she saw, even though she had no idea who was wearing them, and the decorations, and the band, and the food, until finally the subject was exhausted and she could think of nothing more to tell them.

"All right, but tomorrow, when you've had time to think about it some, you must tell it all over again," one of the girls insisted.

"Yes, and also tomorrow, tell us which dress you think was most beautiful."

"I promise," Katie said. "But I have to go upstairs and get some sleep now. It's been a very long and tiring day for me."

"Katie," one of the girls said as Katie started out of the parlor. Katie turned and looked back toward her. "We're really glad you went to the party," the girl said. "Thank you for going, and for sharing it with us."

Katie nodded, feeling a twinge of guilt that she had been able to enjoy the evening while the closest the girls could come was listening to her description of the event. Seeing how important this little contact with the rest of the world was to them, Katie made a private vow that she would give it even more thought tonight. That way, when she renewed her conversation with them again tomorrow, she would be able to make it even more exciting.

She left the parlor and went out into the hallway to the foot of the stairs. Looking toward the kitchen, she happened to see Doc Masters talking to Señor Muñoz, and it wasn't until that moment that she remembered Win had gone over to the Red Bull to rescue Muñoz from a drunken cowboy. Obviously the rescue had been effective, for Muñoz was here.

"Oh, Señor Muñoz, thank goodness you aren't hurt," Katie said, going to him, feeling guilty because she hadn't even thought about him until this moment. "I heard that some drunken cowboy had accosted you."

"*Sí, señorita*, he did. But I am pleased to say that Marshal Coulter put the bad man in jail."

"Good for the marshal. Jail is exactly where such a ruffian should be. And good evening to you, Doc," Katie added. "I didn't mean to overlook you; it's just that I was worried about Señor Muñoz's safety."

"Quite all right," Doc said. "I heard you talking with the other young ladies in the parlor about the cotillion. I am glad you had a good time."

"Yes, thank you. I did have a good time. I wish you had come, Doc. Had you been there, we could have shared a dance."

"Yes, my absence was my misfortune, Miss Skyles," Doc said.

"Perhaps some other time?" Katie said.

"It would be a privilege and an honor," Doc said.

With a parting nod to the two men, she started back toward the stairs. That was when she heard Maggie and Joe coming down, Joe's boots clumping loudly on the stairs.

"Señor Muñoz, I'm so hungry I could eat a mule. You got anything in the kitchen I could eat?" Joe called toward the kitchen.

Muñoz chuckled. "I do not have a mule, *señor*. But for you, I can always find something," he answered.

Joe tossed a casual greeting toward Katie, then headed for the kitchen. Maggie stayed with Katie.

"I'm sorry I wasn't here to meet you when you returned from the party," Maggie said. She turned and walked back up the stairs with Katie, talking to her along the way.

"That's all right. The girls told me you were, uh, working," Katie replied. She still wasn't that comfortable with the concept of sex as working, and that lack of self-confidence showed when she spoke of it, as she was doing now.

Maggie winked. "Honey, sometimes it isn't working, if you know what I mean," she said in a low, throaty voice.

"No, I'm not sure that I do."

"You'll learn someday," Maggie said with a secret smile. "Trust me, my dear. Someday you will definitely learn what it is all about."

Because such talk was embarrassing to her, Katie decided to change the subject.

"Maggie, why do you suppose Doc didn't go to the dance?" she asked. "Do the townspeople have the same disdain for him that they have for the girls who work here?"

Maggie laughed. "Are you asking if the town has disdain for Doc? Honey, it's more likely that Doc has disdain for the town."

"I can believe that about Doc and this town," Katie said. "But what about women? Does Doc have disdain for women as well? I've never seen him with any of the girls who work here. Have you?"

Maggie looked puzzled, as if she, too, had been contemplating the question. "You know, I've wondered about that too," she admitted. "Doc was always one of our regulars, but something happened to him the last time he went to Tucson and it changed him. He doesn't go upstairs with any of the girls anymore."

"What happened?" Katie asked.

"I don't have any idea what it might be."

"And when he came back from Tucson acting differently, you didn't ask him what was wrong?"

"Honey, Doc isn't the kind of man you ask what is wrong. If something is wrong and he wants you to know, he'll tell you. Otherwise it's best to keep your questions to yourself."

"Yes, I can understand that. Doc is such a . . . private person."

At that moment Katie heard someone playing the piano downstairs. The music was beautiful, filling the house with rich, full chords. A lilting melody seemed to weave through the piece like a thread of gold woven into a very fine cloth.

"Oh, my!" Katie gasped. She held her hand up. "Listen to that beautiful music!"

She couldn't believe what she was hearing. She had attended concerts of the finest pianists in the country, and yet she could honestly say that what she was listening to now was as beautiful as any piano concerto she had ever heard.

"Why, that's Mozart," she said in surprise. "That's *Sonata in F major.* Who on earth would have thought that there would be anyone in Epitaph with the musical skills to play so beautifully?"

"Don't you know who that is?" Maggie asked.

Katie shook her head. "I haven't the slightest idea," she answered.

"It's Doc Masters," Maggie said.

"*That* is Doc Masters? I'm amazed. Maggie, that's the playing of an accomplished musician."

"Doc is a skilled musician. Go and see for yourself, if you don't believe me," Maggie said.

Katie walked back to the head of the stairs so she could look down into the parlor. She saw Doc sitting at the piano, leaning toward the keyboard with his head tilted slightly as he played. The girls who had earlier gathered so eagerly around Katie to hear her stories were now sitting about the parlor, on the sofa, on chairs, and even on the floor, listening in rapt silence to the music spilling out of the battered old piano in the parlor.

Katie stood at the head of the stairs, letting the music sweep over her. Never had she heard anything more beautiful . . . it was agony and ecstasy, and it stirred her very soul. She saw, too, that the girls in the parlor were equally moved, for they were wiping their eyes, and even Maggie shed a tear or two.

Was it possible? Katie wondered. Could this be the same man who could call down three armed men and set them run-

ning just from fear of his name? What personal and private
hell had this man been through to bring him to a place like
Epitaph? He could be filling concert halls in New York, Bos-
ton, Philadelphia, and even London and Paris if he wanted to.
Instead, he was sitting in the parlor of a whorehouse in a town
so small that its entire population could fit into one of the
larger concert halls.

Finally the piece ended and Doc poured himself a glass of
whiskey, then played another song, this one light and bouncy,
and more in keeping with the type of music one might expect
in such a place.

With that the mood was broken, and telling Maggie good-
night, Katie let herself into her room, where she went to bed.

Shortly after Katie got into bed, she heard Suzie cry out. It
wasn't a cry of pain or fear. It was a cry of passion.

Katie knew what the cry was because she had heard such
sounds several times since moving into the Courtesan House.
She would lie alone in her room, listening to the sounds of
men and women making love in the rooms closest to hers and
sometimes, in the stillness of the night, she would let wonder
creep into her thoughts.

"Sometimes it isn't work, if you know what I mean," Maggie had said tonight.

Although Katie wasn't sure what she meant, sometimes, in
the recesses of her soul, she admitted to herself that she would
like to know.

She scolded herself, for again she was having erotic
thoughts, thoughts that a few short weeks ago had never even
entered her mind. Now she turned over in bed, hoping to find
some way to block out the sound. But when she did so this
time, she made an amazing discovery!

Katie gasped at what she saw, for there, reflected in the
propped-open transom glass above her door, was the very
thing that had caused Suzie's cry of passion. By some trick of
optical projection, Katie's transom was picking up a reflection
off the transom across the hallway . . . Suzie's transom. And
as clearly as if she were looking in a mirror, Katie could see
into Suzie's room where the lamp was burning brightly and a

scene of wanton passion was being played out upon Suzie's
bed.

The bed coverings had been cast aside and two naked figures were clearly visible. Suzie lay with her legs spread in a
V shape, and Katie could see a dark tangle of hair and a pink,
glistening cleft. The man with her, Billy Kramer, was also
naked. And though Katie had gotten a brief glimpse of Win
Coulter when he was nude, she had never before seen an
aroused, naked man.

"You saw it when it was just hanging there," Suzie had
told her some time later, when Katie had gathered enough
courage to ask about it. "You should see it when a man has
a hard-on, standing out so big and so proud."

Katie had never heard the term *hard-on* before that conversation. She wasn't sure what Suzie meant and she had been
too embarrassed to ask. There was no question now, as to what
she meant, for Billy's manhood wasn't just hanging there. It
was, as Suzie had described, "standing out so big and so
proud."

What Katie saw next, however, made her gasp out loud.
She saw Suzie take Billy into her mouth! It was not something
she would have ever even thought of, and yet, seeing it done
had the most disturbing effect on her. She watched, totally
mesmerized by the scene.

After a while Billy moved his head down to the junction of
Suzie's splayed legs. His mouth paused for a moment over the
dark triangle, then his tongue slipped into that glistening cleft.
Katie grew faint from the sensations she was experiencing. It
was as if fire and ice were being brought together. Her own
breath began coming in gasps, as short and desperate as the
breathing of Suzie and Billy on the bed in the other room.

She was puzzled by the heat she felt. A moment before it
had been cool enough for her to require a blanket. Now she
had to cast the blanket aside because she was being swept by
such heat that she began to perspire. She slipped out of her
sleeping gown and felt an unaccustomed breath of air on her
bare skin, though the breeze did little to cool the heat that now
blazed unchecked.

Steadily, Suzie and Billy's moans grew more urgent while

their thrashing became more frenzied. Then they seemed to reach an apex of some sort, bringing about louder and more intense little cries and grunts from both of them. After that there was a prolonged stillness, and the two lay in each other's arms.

Katie, who was alone in her own bed, felt a sense of emptiness then, and an almost overwhelming desire to experience something like what she had just witnessed. She had heard the sounds before and she had listened to the girls talk, quietly, about things that only they could understand, and she had wondered about it. But now she had been a witness and she didn't have to wonder about it anymore.

Now she knew.

13

ON THE ROAD LEADING INTO EPITAPH FROM THE MCHENRY ranch, Jim McHenry was riding one horse and leading another. Ike Kramer was riding alongside him. They were both accompanying a wagon driven by Ike Kramer and pulled by a team of mules. The wagon was being taken into town. There, the three men planned to disconnect the team and take it back, leaving the wagon and its macabre load parked on Front Street in the middle of Epitaph.

One of the benefits of being a law officer in Epitaph was the unlimited visiting rights Win and Joe had with the girls at the Courtesan House. Maggie had actually given both Win and Joe a key to the front door of the place. Win had taken advantage of this privilege before, but this time when he entered the house, he didn't even bother to visit one of the rooms where he knew he would be welcome.

Instead, he found himself standing outside Katie's door. He knew that she wasn't a soiled dove and there was every chance that she would turn him away. But she was the one he really wanted, and he wasn't going to let the opportunity slip away for lack of trying.

On the other side of the door, Katie, who had not gone back to sleep after witnessing Billy and Suzie in flagrante delicto, heard a light knock. Thinking it might be Suzie, she sat up.

"Suzie?" she called, gently. "Suzie, is that you?"

"No, it's me, Katie. It's Win," a voice replied, softly.

Surprised, Katie got out of bed and padded, barefooted, across the carpet.

"Win, what are *you* doing here?" She opened the door and saw him standing there, dimly illuminated by a splash of light from the lantern at the far end of the hall. She saw, too, the look on his face when he saw her. It was not until that moment that she realized she had not put her sleeping gown back on. To shield herself, she stepped behind the door, then leaned around. Even as she did so she was aware of the change in her frame of reference. Before coming to Epitaph, such an unexpected encounter would have caused her to scream out in alarm and slam the door shut. Now, she just calmly stepped behind the door and asked if anything was wrong.

"No," Win said. He cleared his throat. "I, uh, just thought you might like to know that I didn't get myself killed when I went down to the Red Bull."

"Yes, I saw Señor Muñoz. He was most grateful to you for coming to his aid."

"I'm glad I could help," Win said. He stood at the door, looking past Katie toward the mirror in her room. What Katie didn't know was that though the door shielded her from Win's direct view, he could see her reflection in the mirror, lighted by the hall lantern that invaded her room with a wedge of light stabbing through the partially open door.

"Do you want to come in?" Katie asked. Even as she heard herself forming the words, she couldn't believe she was actually issuing the invitation, for doing so would expose her completely to him, since she had nothing with which to shield her nakedness. And yet she knew that she would be very disappointed if he said no.

"Yes, I think I would like that," Win answered, stepping inside.

When the door closed the light dimmed so that while he could still tell that she was nude, he could see her only by the silver splash of moonlight. He had been surprised by her invitation to come in, and was even more surprised when she stepped toward him, as if inviting him to put his arms around her.

Win did just that, kissing her as he pulled her nude body to him. Katie returned his kiss, then began unbuttoning his shirt until he was standing before her, stripped to the waist.

Win could almost believe that he had come into the wrong room. He could have expected such a reaction from Suzie, or one of the other girls. But from the bookkeeper?

Katie lifted her hands to his face, and he felt her slender fingers traveling slowly down his cheeks, down his neck to his shoulders, and then to his chest. Her mouth followed her fingers as she kissed his shoulder; then he felt the heat of her moist tongue licking it lightly, back and forth across its breadth, sliding downward to his nipple, flicking it, licking it hungrily, hardening it to steel. Then her tongue began wandering over his chest, leaving a mildly chill trail in its wet wake.

Unbuckling his belt, he let his denims drop and in a few more seconds he was as nude as she. Then he scooped her up and carried her over to the bed.

"Win," she said. "I've never done this before."

Win stopped.

"No!" she gasped. "No, please, don't stop! I want this, don't you understand? I want it!"

"You're sure?"

"Yes, please, yes, go on!" she gasped as her searching hand found his erection, then curled cool fingers around the hot skin.

Win's fingers groped for her thighs and, dipping into the moistness, he spread the lips. Now he shifted and was on top of her. Her hand grabbed his cock and she guided it into her, taking it slowly, until it was stopped by the physical evidence of her virginity. There, he hesitated.

"No, don't stop, don't stop!" she whimpered. She put her hands on the cheeks of his butt then, and pulled him into her, full length, grunting once as she experienced the pain of the first time.

Win realized then that whatever sting there might have been must have dissipated quickly, for she began gyrating, rotating around his cock, finding its throbbing head with every nerve ending within. He drove into her, deep, hard, and fast, their bellies slapping against each other with smacking sounds, the bed squeaking from the action until, finally, they came together. When they did so, Katie squealed ecstatically.

She paused, only for a moment, then quickly resumed her gyrating, thrusting upward as she ground against him with renewed vigor. So aggressive was she that Win's cock had no time to slacken, but continued as hard as before.

Katie was like some wild creature.

Win had experienced all sorts of women, all ages, all sizes, all shapes, and with all manner of talents. But no woman, regardless of her experience, had ever exploded around him with the reckless abandon of this innocent virgin.

Win came again, and if the squeal of joy escaping her lovely mouth signaled orgasm on her part, Katie did as well. When at last Win pulled out of her, he saw with some embarrassment that he was as limp as a wet noodle.

And yet still Katie wanted more. Going down on him she licked and nipped, sucked and chewed, whipping its head with her tireless tongue, bringing it back to rigidity one more time, despite its previous exhaustion. And when, once again, she got it up and ready, she took nearly half of it into her mouth, closing her lips snugly around it, and punishing the head with the warm, moist walls behind her tongue.

It wasn't until he finally came again, shooting one last weak load, that she slowly loosened her lips, and let him slip free.

Always an early riser, Joe walked through the predawn darkness toward the town marshal's office, where he planned to put on a pot of coffee. He was already hungry, but the coffee would have to hold him until the Alhambra opened for breakfast.

He saw a wagon ahead and at first thought it was sitting in front of the apothecary next door. When he got a little closer, though, he realized that the wagon was actually parked in front of the marshal's office, a situation he found curious. The fact that there was no team attached to the wagon made the situation even more curious, so he quickened his pace to see what it was about.

When he reached the wagon he saw that it wasn't empty.

There was something in the back, covered by a tarpaulin. Joe grabbed a corner of the tarpaulin and pulled it to one side.

"Son of a bitch!" he said aloud.

There were six men in the wagon. All six were riddled with bullets . . . and all six were dead. One of the six was Kyle Rawlings.

When J. C. Malone went down to the hardware store, where the bodies had been taken, he had them strapped to one-by-six planks and propped up against the front of the store so he could take their pictures. The sight of so many bodies in one place drew a rather sizable crowd and they stood around in curiosity, watching Malone work.

Malone, ever the good newspaper man, got the pictures, which he would display in the front window of the newspaper office, as well as the story.

BLOODY RANGE BATTLE
Fight Over Stolen Cattle
Six Are Killed

On the 5th, while most citizens of the city and county were enjoying a wonderful dance party sponsored by the Epitaph Cotillion Committee, the Grim Reaper wrought a terrible carnage out on the range.

Rancher Kyle Rawlings, convinced that his cattle had been stolen by the Kramers and the McHenrys, and unable to find satisfaction from the county sheriff's department, did what any self-respecting man would do. He took matters into his own hands. Leading a party of his own men to the McHenry ranch, Rawlings was bent upon recovering his stolen cattle. The visit was made in the middle of the night, with the intent of using the cover of darkness.

To the great misfortune and ultimate doom of Kyle Rawlings and those brave lads who rode with him, however, the McHenrys were warned by Deputy Sheriff Deekus Taggart of their approach. With neighbor Ike Kramer and no fewer than eight armed men, the McHenrys waited until the riders were in their midst.

At this point there is some confusion as to what happened. Ike Kramer says that a warning was called out to the would-be cattle thieves, and they were given the opportunity to throw down their arms and return to their own ranch, empty-handed. Other sources have insisted to this newspaper, however, that no warning was given. Instead, the defenders opened fire from their position in ambuscade, sending deadly missiles of death through the darkness.

It was not a battle as much as it was a slaughter, and the results were, predictably, very lopsided. For those who waited in ambush at the McHenry ranch—Ike Kramer, Jim and Frank McHenry, and the armed men who were at their side—not one wound was sustained. But for Kyle Rawlings and the brave young men who rode with him on that fateful night, it was their last moment on earth, as all were killed.

Two days after Kyle, Slim, Parker, and the others were buried, Ike Kramer hired a lawyer from Tucson to file a claim in circuit court against Kyle's ranch. Billy was uncomfortable with the claim and told Ike as much, but when the claim was presented, it included Billy as one of the plaintiffs.

"Sally Kramer's will plainly stated that Kyle Rawlings must operate the ranch for ten years," Ike's lawyer said in his presentation to the judge. "He clearly did not do so, and thus the land and all property, fixed and movable, must return to Ike and Billy Kramer."

There were many in the town who thought it seemed unfair,

pointing out that Kyle didn't operate the ranch for ten years because Ike killed him before the ten years was up.

However, it was also pointed out that Kyle's death had already been ruled as a justifiable homicide. And, while there were several who didn't like Ike Kramer and wanted to see him fail in his lawsuit, there was really no one to argue the case against him, since Kyle Rawlings had left no known survivors. Thus, regardless of how unpopular his decision might be, the judge had no choice but to rule in favor of Ike and Billy Kramer. The Rawlings land, and all property, fixed and movable, was awarded to Ike and Billy Kramer.

The piano in the Red Bull was playing merrily, but the noise in the saloon was such that no one could hear it from more than ten feet away. In one corner, Ike, Jim, and Frank, and a few cowboys, including Asa Blanchard, were singing in competition with the piano. They had been drinking and singing in celebration of the judge's order ever since the order was handed down.

When Doc came into the saloon after supper, he saw that it was much too noisy for any kind of a serious card game, so he stepped up to the bar.

"Hello, Doc," the bartender asked. "Your usual?"

"Yes, thanks, Sam," Doc replied.

Sam pulled a bottle of aged bourbon from beneath the bar. It was a brand that he kept on hand especially for Doc, and kept under the bar just for him. He poured Doc a drink, put the bottle back under the bar, then returned to rubbing his rag on the bar. If anyone had asked Sam, he would have told them he was cleaning the bar. In reality he was just spreading the spilled liquor around, which did nothing toward improving the bar surface. The bar still reflected the scars inflicted upon it by the shotgun blast of Charley Pearl when he'd tried to kill Win Coulter on the first day Win and Joe arrived.

Doc turned his back to the bar to look out over the raucous celebration.

"How long have they been at it?" he asked.

"Ever since they come out of court this afternoon," Sam said. "Don't know why the McHenrys are celebratin' so. Ike

Kramer is the only one who gained by it. Well, Ike and Billy.''

"Has Billy been in here?"

"No," Sam answered. "If you ask me, he's a little shamed by the whole thing."

"Hey! Hey!" Ike shouted to the others, after taking another long pull on a bottle of whiskey. "Are we just goin' to sit around here suckin' on a bottle like a baby on a tit, or are we all goin' over to the Courtesan House?"

"Now, Ike, you know we ain't welcome at the Courtesan House," Frank said, shaking his finger back and forth. "The McHenrys and the Kramers just ain't welcome there."

"That ain't true," Jim said. "Us McHenrys ain't welcome, 'n' ole Ike here ain't welcome. But little Billy boy? Why, he's welcome as rain. Why is that, Ike? Why is Billy welcome and you ain't?"

" 'Cause Billy's got good manners," Ike said. "He's my little brother and I raised him up proper."

"Too bad you didn't learn some of them manners yourself. If you had some of 'em, maybe we wouldn't get turned away ever' time we tried to get into that fancy whorehouse."

"We'll get in there tonight," Ike said.

"Yeah? What makes you think so?"

" 'Cause I'm celebratin', and I don't intend to get turned away tonight," Ike answered. "And if you're men, you'll go with me. All of you," he said, taking in the handful of cowboys who had been a part of the celebration all day.

"Sure, why not?" Jim said. "Hell, I'll go with you." He stood up, drained the last of the bottle and tossed it over his head casually. It hit the corner of the bar, then smashed into little pieces, but the three men didn't even look around at it as they stepped outside.

"They's goin' to be a shootin' for sure," someone said. "I seen both the Coulters down there a while ago."

"Come on, let's go watch!" another said, and a moment later there was a mad rush for the doors.

"Doc, you'd better . . ." Sam started, then stopped when he saw that Doc was no longer standing at the bar.

•   •   •

Word had preceded the crowd, so that by the time Ike and
those with him reached the Courtesan House, Win and Joe
were already standing on the front porch of the house. They
stood there like unmovable statues as the crowd arrived from
the saloon, then arrayed itself in a half circle around the front.

Ike Kramer, Jim and Frank McHenry, and the three cowboys who had been with them were standing in the dirt of the
street, looking up. The only light came from a kerosene lamp
that gleamed from the wall right behind the Coulters. It cast
a golden bubble of light that splashed out into the street, making deep shadows on the faces of everyone present.

"I believe you gentlemen have come to a place where you
are not wanted," Win said, speaking in a low, quiet voice, all
the more menacing because of its apparent lack of emotion.

"Get out of the way, Coulter," Ike called. "Me 'n' my
friends is comin' in." In contrast, Ike's voice was loud and
threatening. "You got that, Win Coulter? We're comin' in."

"No, I don't think so, Kramer," Win answered as calmly
as before.

"What makes you think we ain't?"

"Because we won't let you," Win replied.

"Yeah? Well, the only way you gonna stop us is to shoot
us," Ike said. "And there's six of us and only two of you."

"Make that three," another voice said. Doc Masters appeared from the dark, then stepped up onto the porch and
turned to face the crowd.

"All right, so there are three of you. We still outnumber
you two to one," Ike blustered. "You really want to fight it
out with us?"

"Yes, I do," Win said. "I'm ready to settle the issue right
here and right now." He dropped his arm loosely to his side.
One of the three cowboys who had come with Ike and the
McHenrys was Asa Blanchard. "Blanchard, are you dealing
yourself into this hand?"

All conversation halted then, and there was a collective
holding of breath as the crowd waited for the play to unfold.

"No," Blanchard suddenly said. "No, I was just out to have
a little fun, that's all. I . . . I don't want no part of this." He
put his hands up in the air. "Marshal, when the shooting starts,

I ain't goin' to be a part of it," he added, backing away slowly.

"Me neither," one of the others said, and, cautiously, the other two cowboys joined the first.

"Well, Kramer, what do you say?" Win baited. "Are we going to do this or not?"

"What's goin' on down here?" another voice asked. "You folks, break it up. Break it up and go on home," the voice said authoritatively.

The voice belonged to Sheriff Bean, who moved through the crowd, shoving people roughly to one side or the other.

"All right, all right, Sheriff," Ike suddenly said, holding his hands out in front of him to show that he was not about to make a hostile move. "We ain't goin' to draw. Put your hands out, boys," he said to the others. "If anything happens, Sheriff, it's the Coulters' doin's. We ain't goin' to draw."

"Go on home now, boys, the show is over," Bean said to the gathered crowd when Ike and the McHenrys had walked away without unsheathing their weapons.

"What the hell did you butt in for?" Win asked as the crowd began disappearing into the darkness.

"Hell, somebody had to take a hand," Bean said. "Things was startin' to get out of control."

"Yeah, well, I was about to put things back into control," Win said.

"How did you plan to do that?"

"I was going to kill them," Win answered unequivocally.

14

OUT IN THE *BARRIO* DEEKUS TAGGART WAS FRUSTRATED. Everywhere he went he encountered bands of men carrying rifles, shotguns, or pistols. Some were carrying pikes, long poles to which had been attached wicked-looking knives. In twos and threes they were walking the streets and the alleys, or standing outside the houses and the cantina.

"*Buenas noches*, Señor Deputy," one of them said as Taggart walked down the main street.

"Who is that?" Taggart asked, staring into the dark.

"It is I, Señor Deputy. Ricardo Bustamante."

"Bustamante," Taggart said. "Yes, I know you." Taggart waved his hand, taking in the street. "Tell me, Bustamante, what is all this about? Why are so many armed men walking around?"

"*El Bestia, señor,*" Bustamante said.

"*El Bestia?*"

"The Beast," Bustamante explained. "The creature that is half human and half animal, who comes in the night to kill our women." He held up his shotgun. "When he comes again, we will kill him."

"If he is what you say he is, do you think you can kill him with a gun?" Taggart asked.

"*Sí*, with the help of Jesus." Bustamante held out the crucifix he was wearing. "*El Bestia* will not attack someone who is protected by the *crucifijo*."

"Ha, a lot of good that will do you. Maria Sanchez was wearing a cross."

"No, *señor*, I do not think so," Bustamante answered. "None were wearing a cross when they were found."

"Oh. I guess I just thought all Mexican women wore a cross. Well, good luck in your search for *El Bestia*."

"Gracias, señor."

Unable to slip through the band of armed men, Taggart returned to his room. He took the box from under his bed and opened it, then fingered each of his souvenirs, but that wasn't enough. His chest felt tight, his breathing was hard, and he burned with an unbearable heat. Never had his need been stronger than it was right now, yet there was nothing he could do about it. Nearly every man in the *barrio* was armed and looking out for the one they called The Beast. Even the whores, who used to ply their trade alone, were now sticking together. It was beginning to look like it would be impossible for Taggart to find any more relief in the *barrio*.

With shaking hands, Taggart poured himself a whiskey. It took three drinks before an idea began to germinate. Then, once he knew what he was going to do, the shaking stopped. He put his totems back in the box, slid it under the bed, and left his room, walking out into the night to put his plan into operation.

Win and Joe were having breakfast when Martin Jackson came into the Alhambra. Since he was a member of the town council, a visit from Jackson didn't seem all that unusual to them. But this morning Jackson was wearing his high hat and a dark jacket with tails—his undertaking garb.

"What is it, Jackson?" Win asked. "Why the get-up?"

Jackson looked at the brothers with an expression of practiced solemnity.

"I'm afraid I have some bad news," he said. "The one who has been killing the Mexican whores, the ones they call *El Bestia*, has struck again. This time, on our side of the tracks."

"One of the cribs?" Win asked. "One of the girls who work the catbird seats?"

Jackson shook his head. "No," he said. "I'm afraid it is Miss Maggie DeShay herself."

"What?" Joe asked, standing up so quickly that his chair fell over. Everyone else in the restaurant looked over at him in curiosity. "Are you telling me Maggie is dead?"

The words buzzed around the restaurant as they were passed from table to table.

"Teresa found her this morning," Jackson said. "She was in her own bed, with her throat cut."

"Son of a bitch!" Joe said. He shook his head. "Son of a bitch! Who could do such a thing?"

By the time Win and Joe reached the Courtesan House, a crowd of solemn onlookers had gathered around outside. They stood on the side of the street, on the lawn, along the edges of the flower beds, and up on the front porch, but none of them had gone inside. They parted to let Win and Joe in.

Inside, all the girls were gathered in the parlor, and all were crying. Katie, seeing Win and Joe, came over to them. She went into Win's arms and cried into his chest. Suzie came to Joe.

"Oh, Joe, you were Maggie's favorite. If only you had been with her last night," Suzie said.

"Did anyone hear anything, or see anything?" Joe asked.

"Not a sight, not a sound," Suzie answered. "We've already talked among ourselves, and we don't have any idea who it was."

"Win, do you think there is a chance you can find out who did this terrible thing?" Katie asked.

"I don't know," Win admitted. "There is always a chance, but, like I told you, my brother and I aren't really lawmen."

"You will try, though?"

"Yes, of course we will try."

"I had no idea how much I would miss her," Katie said. "She was my . . . my anchor, out here."

One of those most devastated by Maggie's death was the maid, Teresa. She was standing over in a corner, alone, sobbing out loud.

"Look at poor Teresa," Katie said. "She seems to be taking it harder than any of us."

Katie and Win walked over to comfort Teresa.

"Teresa, are you all right?"

"Oh, Señorita Skyles," Teresa said. "Señorita DeShay was such a good woman. I know she was a sinner, but she was a good woman. I have said many times the Rosary, and I have prayed that God will not send her to hell. Do you think He will?"

"If you were God, would you send her to hell?" Katie asked.

Teresa crossed herself quickly. "No," she said.

"Why not?"

"Because I know her. She was a soiled dove, yes, but she was a good woman. I know her."

"Don't you think God knows her as well? And don't you think He is as forgiving?"

"Oh, *sí, sí!*" Theresa said. She crossed herself again. "*Sí,* I think maybe you are right."

"I just cannot imagine who could do something like this," Katie said.

"It was *El Bestia*," Teresa said. "The one who is half animal and half man."

"It was a beast, all right," Win said. "But this beast is only a man."

Andrew Henson came into the parlor then. Katie knew that he was Maggie's lawyer because, as Maggie's accountant, she had discussed some business with him. Now he came over to see her.

"Mr. Henson, isn't it awful?" Katie asked.

"Yes, it is terrible," Henson agreed. He cleared his throat. "Miss Skyles, I hate to bring up business at such a time, but I shall require your signature in at least half a dozen places. Perhaps we could go back into the dining room for a few moments? I'll lay all the papers out for you."

"My signature? What papers?"

"Oh, I'm sorry," Henson said. "You and Maggie were so

close, and of course you were handling most of her business.
I just assumed you knew.''

"Knew what, Mr. Henson?"

"About Maggie's will, Miss Skyles. Maggie DeShay named
you as sole beneficiary to her entire estate. You have inherited
all of her money, and the Courtesan House.''

Maggie's funeral was conducted three days later. The procession to the cemetery was a stately affair that Katie felt certain
would have pleased Maggie. Maggie's black and silver coffin
rested behind the glass panels of the hearse, while two liveried
coachmen drove a matching team of black horses to pull the
funeral coach. Hundreds of people lined the streets on both
sides, and they doffed their hats in respect as the procession
passed them by.

Katie, Suzie, and the other girls from the Courtesan House
rode in two open carriages just behind the hearse. She and the
others dabbed at their eyes openly and unashamedly as the
solemn procession moved along the streets of the town.

Boot Hill was a drab and dreary place. It was on a hill that
overlooked the town of Epitaph. It was completely barren, and
grave sites were often marked by nothing more than a carpet
of pebbles and rocks. Here and there were wooden head mark-
ers, but there were no granite monuments of the type that
marked the graves of Katie's parents back in Memphis.

The grave had already been opened, the dirt alongside the
hole white from the sun, though it had only been exposed for
little more than an hour. The marker right next to the hole that
was about to become Maggie's grave was that of Lucien
Thompkins. It was not until Maggie's will was read that the
town found out a secret that Maggie had kept all this time.

Maggie DeShay was actually Maggie Thompkins, the
widow of the man who had brought the theater group to Epitaph so long ago.

Those who had come to mourn at Maggie's funeral now
gathered around the grave as Father Tuttle, the Episcopal
priest and the only clergyman in town who would agree to
conduct the funeral of a harlot, began his graveside homily.

"It is," the priest said, "perhaps fitting that this woman

was known in life as Maggie, for the name Maggie, taken from Margaret, means 'woman of Magdala.' Once there was another woman of Magdala, a woman named Mary.''

The priest paused for a moment to allow his words to sink in. A hot breath of air moved through the cemetery, pushing before it a cloud of dust that stung the faces of the mourners.

''Like our Maggie, Mary of Magdala was a locally notorious woman with a bad name in the town. But she came purposefully to make an act of penitence to Jesus, and she stood behind him at his feet, weeping so that she wet his feet with her tears. And she wiped his feet with the hair of her head, and she kissed his feet and then she anointed them with ointment.

''Now there was a Pharisee named Simon, in whose house this happened. Simon thought ill of the woman and he looked on in disapproval, but Jesus said to Simon, 'Do you see this woman? I entered your house, you gave me no water for my feet, but she has wet my feet with her tears, and wiped them with her hair. You gave me no kiss, but from the time I came in she has not ceased to kiss my feet. You did not anoint my head with oil, but she has anointed my feet with ointment. Therefore I tell you, her sins, which are many, are forgiven, for she loved much, but he who loves little, is forgiven little.' And then Jesus said to Mary of Magdala, 'Your sins are forgiven. Your faith has saved you. Go in peace.' ''

The priest looked at the coffin that contained Maggie's body, and made the sign of the cross over it.

''Maggie DeShay, your sins are forgiven. The love you had for others has saved you. Go in peace.''

Maggie's coffin was lowered into the grave then, and the priest picked up a handful of dirt and dropped it into the grave. The dirt made a drumming sound as it hit the lid of the casket.

''In sure and certain hope of the resurrection to eternal life through our Lord Jesus Christ, we commend to Almighty God our sister Maggie DeShay, and we commit her body to the ground; earth to earth, ashes to ashes, dust to dust.''

The funeral ended shortly after that, and the mourners began returning to the horses, carriages, buggies, and wagons that had brought them up here. Win, Joe, Katie, and Suzie had

driven up in a rented buckboard. As they climbed into the
buckboard for the ride back to town they could hear, behind
them, the sound of the dirt leaving the spade as the hole was
closed.

There was a brooding mood in Epitaph. Win perceived it the
moment they reached the edge of town. It was something he
could sense in the air, like the heavy feel of the atmosphere
just before a storm.

"Joe?" It was an unasked question, but Joe needed no more
than the one word, for he understood.

"Yeah," Joe answered. "I know. Something is up."

"What is it?" Katie asked. "What are you two talking
about?"

They saw two young boys running along the board sidewalk, jumping over the stoops and doorsills as they hurried
toward the center of town.

"Hey, you boys! What's the hurry?" Win shouted.

"We're goin' to see the stretchin'!" one of the boys called
back in excitement.

"Stretching?" Katie asked.

"Damn, there's a lynchin' goin' on!" Joe shouted. He was
driving and he slapped the reins hard against the team to urge
them into a gallop.

In no time the buckboard made it to the far end of the street;
then, using his left foot, Joe pushed hard on the brake lever
while he hauled back on the reins. The buckboard slid to a
stop.

"Ole Muñoz never looked so good," someone on the edge
of the crowd said in a high, nervous voice. Someone else gig-
gled.

"What is it?" Win asked. "What's going on here?"

The crowd began parting to allow Win and the others to
pass through. When he got to the front of the crowd he saw
what had drawn them here. Señor Muñoz was hanging from
a crosspiece that had been nailed between two telegraph poles.
The old cook's hands were tied behind his back and his neck
was grotesquely stretched out of shape. He had not been blind-
folded and his eyes were open, as if staring accusingly at his

lynchers. The rope creaked as Muñoz swung slowly back and forth on the makeshift gallows.

"My God!" Katie said, putting her hand over her mouth. "Who did this?"

"A group of Maggie's friends," someone in the crowd answered. "They did it for Maggie."

"For Maggie? You did this for Maggie? You are mad, all of you!"

Win and Joe said nothing more as they drove Katie and Suzie back to the Courtesan House. Letting them out there, they then drove down to the Jingle Bell Corral, where they turned in the buckboard and the team. From there, they walked across the street to the Red Bull Saloon.

"Yes, sir," Blanchard was saying. He put his finger to the side of his head. "I started thinkin' on it, and I got it all figured out. Who else coulda been killing them Mexican whores but Muñoz? I mean, he was Mexican, wasn't he? That means he could go anywhere down there he wanted to without anyone paying him any mind.

"Well, it was one thing him killing the Mexican whores, but when he started in on our whores, I figured somethin' had to be done about it. And we damn sure wasn't goin' to get nothin' done by our two marshals."

"So you decided to kill Muñoz yourself, is that it?" Win asked.

"You damn right I . . ." Blanchard started to answer, but when he saw that Win was the one who asked the question, he clammed up. "Coulter," he said. "What are you doing here?"

"I'm going to throw your ass in jail," Win said. "And you're going to stay there for about three days."

"Three days," Blanchard snorted. "And what's going to happen in three days?"

"We're going to see another hanging," Win replied. "Only this time it's going to be legal."

"Who do you think you're kidding?" Blanchard asked. "You ain't goin' to be able to put together a jury in this town that will hang me for what I done. Hell, half of 'em was out there, eggin' me on!''

"Then I'll hang you myself," Win said, flatly. "Either way, you're going to hang."

"The hell I am!" Blanchard shouted. He pulled his gun, even as he was shouting his defiance. Win had not yet pulled his gun, but Blanchard had his out and was coming back on the hammer even as Win started for his pistol. Win turned as he drew, presenting a sideways profile, rather than the broader, front profile. That action saved his life, for Blanchard pulled the trigger at about the same time Win was bringing his own gun up, and the bullet missed Win by less than an inch. Had Win been in a full frontal presentation, the bullet would have hit him in the heart.

Blanchard thumbed the hammer back for a second shot, already correcting for his error, when Win fired. Win's bullet crashed into Blanchard's heart, killing him so quickly that he was dead before he hit the floor.

"Drop your gun, Coulter!" a loud voice called.

Looking into the recently replaced mirror behind the bar, Win saw Sheriff Bean and Deputy Sheriff Taggart. Both men were holding shotguns, and the guns were pointed at Win and Joe.

"What's this about?" Win asked.

"I said, *drop the gun!*" Bean repeated. "You too," he added, talking to Joe. "Unbuckle your gun belt. There will be no more taking the law into your own hands."

"Where were you this afternoon when this son of a bitch lynched Muñoz?" Win asked.

"Lynched Muñoz? Far as I'm concerned he just saved the county the cost of a legal hanging," Bean said. "He was right. Muñoz was the killer."

"How do you know that?"

"Because I seen him comin' out of the whorehouse around two o'clock in the mornin' on the night Maggie DeShay was killed," Taggart said.

"That proves nothing. He worked there."

"He was a cook. He had no business bein' there at that time of night," Bean said.

"Yeah, well, even if he did do it, and I don't believe he did, Blanchard had no right to hang him."

"I know that," Bean said. "That's why we came over here. We was goin' to arrest him and put him on trial. But we got here too late. You'd already killed him. So now we'll just put you on trial."

"Don't worry, Win," Sam Norton said. "They's enough of us in here seen what really happened, and when Judge Spicer hears our side of it, he'll let you go in a minute."

"Let's go," Bean said, making a motion with his shotgun. "You know what I think I'm goin' to do? I'm goin' to lock you up in the county jail." He laughed. "Yeah, I like that. Town Marshals Win and Joe Coulter, locked up in the county jail."

Blanchard was buried the next afternoon. Win stood at the side window of the cell, the only window that afforded a view of the street, and watched as the hearse rolled slowly toward the cemetery.

Ike and Billy Kramer, Jim and Frank McHenry, and two dozen or more cowboys walked along behind the hearse, all of them wearing a black mourning band around their arms.

"I'll be damned," Joe said. "Look at that." He pointed to a sign on the hearse.

Asa P. Blanchard,
A Cowboy foully murdered
by
Win Coulter.

15

JUDGE SPICER SET THE TRIAL FOR ONE WEEK LATER, AND ON the day of the trial, two men who were to have a role to play arrived on the morning train. One of the two men was J. Warren Pratt, a prosecuting attorney known throughout the West as the man who prosecuted cases in Judge Isaac Charles Parker's federal court at Fort Smith, Arkansas. Judge Parker's swift justice had resulted in so many hangings that he became known far and wide as "the hanging judge." That reputation rested somewhat on the successful prosecution of the cases that came before him, and that prosecution had been carried out by J. Warren Pratt.

Warren Pratt dressed in a three-piece suit and carried a silver-headed cane. He wore a diamond stickpin in his tie, solid gold cufflinks, and a gold watch chain stretching across the silk vest that did little to conceal his substantial girth. Like his mentor, Judge Parker he had affected a van dyke beard. He kept his hair cut short, and neatly combed.

The other person to arrive was George Maledon, and whenever he entered a town, mothers shuddered and pulled their children close to them.

Maledon was a very small, full-bearded man who always carried a brace of hand-woven, well-oiled, expensive Kentucky hemp ropes with him. He was a professional hangman who had carried out more than fifty death sentences, and had been dubbed "the prince of hangmen."

Though Sheriff Bean had arrested Win and Joe, Doc had persuaded Judge Spicer to move them from the county jail, which was under Bean's administration, to the town jail. And, because Win and Joe were the town marshals, Spicer managed to get U.S. Marshal Truman Algood brought in to take charge of the prisoners until the trial.

When Henson walked into the jail shortly after the prosecutor and the hangman arrived, he saw Win, Doc, Joe, and Marshal Algood sitting around a card table, playing poker.

"Mr. Henson," Algood said. "Have you ever played poker with this man?" He nodded toward Win.

"I can't say that I have," Henson replied.

"I think he cheats," Algood said. "I think we ought to put him in jail."

"I *am* in jail," Win said, laughing.

"Oh, yes, so you are." Algood said. "Well, good enough for you. I fold."

Win took the hand and raked in the pot, which consisted of a dozen or more matches. He looked over at Henson and smiled. "How goes the fight for justice?" he asked.

"It may be more difficult than we thought," Henson answered.

"How can it be? Self-defense is self-defense."

"Pratt has witnesses who will testify that you once shot Blanchard in the foot without provocation. Did you?"

"Hell, no, I was plenty provoked," Win replied, and he, Joe, and Doc laughed.

Henson cleared his throat. "Yes, well, according to Pratt, that created such an atmosphere of fear and distrust that Blanchard could never be sure, any time he saw you, but what you might shoot him again. Thus, as he believed his life was in danger, he was fully justified in drawing against you."

"Well, all right, justified or not, he drew against me, first."

Henson shook his head. "No," he said. "If Pratt proves his case, your very presence was enough of a threat to make Blanchard fear for his life. Thus, you are the aggressor. And as the aggressor, you are guilty of murder."

"What about Joe? He didn't do anything."

"They will get him for aiding and abetting," Henson said.

Win drummed his fingers on the table. "Well," he said. "Thanks for coming to cheer me up."

"There's, uh, more," Henson said.

"By all means, let's have all of it."

"You'll have to leave the jail to see it."

"Hell, that's no problem for me," Win said, smiling broadly. "I'd be glad to leave the jail."

With U.S. Marshal Truman Algood acting as the guard, and with their word of honor as their only restraint, Win and Joe left the jail and walked with Doc, Henson, and the U.S. marshal to see what Henson had to show them.

It was a hangman's gallows.

A few dozen people were standing around watching the construction. A large hand-lettered sign stood in front of the gallows:

On this Gallows, The Master Executioner,
George Maledon,
The Prince Of Hangmen,
Will Hang
Win Coulter
and
Joe Coulter.
These Two Murderers Will Be
Prosecuted by J. Warren Pratt
And Legally Sent To Meet Their Maker
Admission is Free.

Ike Kramer was supervising the construction of the gallows. A ladder of thirteen steps led up to the gallows floor, which was made of freshly cut one-by-eight-inch planks. The tree of the gallows was constructed of four-by-four timbers—three uprights and one crosspiece at the top. Two ropes hung from the crosstree, one on either side of the center brace. The ropes were made of twenty strands of the finest hemp, one-and-a-half inches in circumference. Sandbags were tied to the ropes and two chairs had been placed invitingly on the twenty-foot square with a placard on each chair, one for Win Coulter and the other for Joe Coulter.

The platform looked solid, but Win could see that it had two ominous divisions supported by upright timbers. When those timbers were knocked out of place, the front part of the platform would swing down on hinges and the feet of anyone who had been standing there would be left dangling in midair, the falls broken only by a rope around the neck.

At this moment there were two one-hundred-pound weights on the platform. Ike stepped back from the edge.

"Okay, try it!" Ike shouted.

The two muscular men beneath the platform swung heavy hammers at the supporting posts. The posts were knocked away and the long, narrow trap fell open. The two weights dropped for a short distance, then were jerked up short by the rope.

Seeing Win and Joe, Ike bounded down the steps, calling out to them, "Hey, Coulters! Come to see your gallows, did you? How do you like it?"

"What are you doing here, Kramer?" Marshal Algood asked.

"Why, I'm doing my civic duty," Ike said. He took in the gallows with a wave of his hand. "I have volunteered to foot all the expenses of the hanging. I'm the one brought Maledon in here. I'm payin' him two hundred and fifty dollars per neck, plus all his expenses."

"You have no right to build this damn thing, or to bring in a hangman," Algood said.

"I'm rentin' this empty lot," Ike said. "That makes me the proprietor, and I can build any kind of construction here that I want. I choose to build a gallows."

"You are inflaming the passions of the people," Henson said.

"You damn right I'm inflaming the passions of the people," Kramer replied. "That's what I was planning on doin'."

"I'll get a court order to have it taken down."

"Hell, that don't make any difference to me. Ever'one's seen it by now. And if I take it down, I'll just leave it in pieces so it can be put back together again, real easy. Besides, you can't get no court order to have Maledon run out of town, and ever'where he goes people will see him 'n' they'll know why he's here."

"Let him leave it up," Win said. "When this is all over, I might use it to hang *him*."

When he heard Win's calm words, the smile left Ike's face.

"Oyez, oyez, oyez, the Fourth Circuit Court of the Territory of Arizona is now in session, the Honorable Judge Wells Spicer presiding. All rise!"

Everyone in the courtroom rose as the judge emerged from his chambers and walked over to the bench. When he was seated, the gallery was invited to sit as well and there was a rustle of clothes and a squeak of boots and shoes as the spectators got themselves settled. The courtroom was packed. Admission had been granted on a first-come, first-seated basis, and some people had been outside the courtroom since before dawn.

Katie was in the first row of the gallery, and Suzie and Doc were sitting with her. Also sitting in the same row, but on the other side of the center aisle, were Ike and Billy Kramer, Jim and Frank McHenry, and a handful of witnesses who were going to testify for the prosecution. Win and Joe were seated at the defendants' table with their lawyer, Andrew Henson.

Judge Spicer removed his wire-rimmed glasses and polished them industriously for a moment, holding them up to the light of the window and staring through the lenses, then polishing them even more vigorously. During this ritual of cleaning and polishing there was total silence in the court. Finally, Judge Spicer deemed his glasses clean enough, or perhaps he just considered the mood in the court somber enough, because he put his glasses back on, hooking them very carefully over one ear at a time. Then he fixed a long, studied stare upon the courtroom and cleared his throat.

"The Territory of Arizona versus Win Coulter and Joe Coulter," he said. "Is the prosecution ready?"

J. Warren Pratt stood, put one hand inside his silk vest, then looked over toward the jury.

"Ready, Your Honor," he said in a deep, resonant voice.

"Is the defense ready?"

"Yes, Your Honor," Henson replied, half rising from his chair.

Pratt began to make his case then, using a parade of witnesses who testified as to the demeanor of the town marshals. Witnesses testified that Win had killed Charley Pearl and Vernon Mathis on the very first day they had arrived in town, and though they conceded that it was a fair fight, they said it was a demonstration not only of the marshal's skill with a gun, but of his willingness to kill.

They testified that the Coulters had immediately become friendly with Doc Masters, the only other person in town with sufficient skill with a gun to act as a balance to the reign of terror the Coulters had brought upon the town.

Witnesses also testified that Win and Joe Coulter, as well as Doc Masters, had harassed, threatened, and beaten Ike Kramer and Jim and Frank McHenry.

"I object, Your Honor. This testimony is irrelevant," Henson said.

"On the contrary, Your Honor," Pratt defended. "It is all part and parcel of the picture I am painting of the marshals, Win and Joe Coulter. It is validation of the fact that the behavior of these two men was brutal and profane, even with men of position and wealth. And if that is so, then how much more ruthless and debasing could it be to a poor cowboy of no consequence, such as Asa Blanchard?"

"Objection overruled," Judge Spicer said. "You may continue."

Pratt's next witness was Sheriff Bean, who testified not about the shooting, but about the night Asa Blanchard, Ike Kramer, and Jim and Frank McHenry tried to enter the Courtesan House, only to be stopped by Win, Joe, and Doc.

"And when you arrived on the scene to bring order to what was obviously a volatile situation, there was an exchange between you and the defendant Win Coulter. Would you share that conversation with the court?"

"Be glad to," Bean replied. "Coulter asked me why did I butt in? I told him, 'Hell, somebody had to take a hand. Things was startin' to get out of control.' He said. 'Yeah, well, I was about to put things back into control.' I asked him how did he plan to do that?"

"And what was his answer?" Pratt asked.

Sheriff Bean looked over at the defendants' table.

"He said, just as calm and cold as if it was nothin', 'I was going to kill them,' " Bean answered.

There was a collective gasp of surprise from the court as Pratt walked back over to his own table and shuffled through a few papers before calling his last witness.

The last witness for the prosecution testified about the night that Win had shot Blanchard in the foot. Nothing was mentioned about Blanchard's previously threatening to kill Señor Muñoz.

"I have no further witnesses, Your Honor," Pratt said, sitting down after he excused the final witness.

There was another collective gasp of surprise from those in the court. Pratt had called witnesses who testified about three months of events and behavior, but he did not call one person to give testimony about the actual shooting in which Blanchard was killed.

Now it was time for the defense attorney to make his case. Henson called his own parade of witnesses to the stand, matching the prosecution's witnesses, man for man. Whereas all of Pratt's witnesses had been cowboys, Henson called only those men who lived and worked in the town. Among Henson's witnesses were the mayor and two members of the town council, all of whom told the court that they had gone to ask Win and Joe Coulter to take the job of town marshal.

"And are you sorry you asked them, now?" Henson asked. He asked the same question of all three, and all three answered the same way.

"I am not in the least sorry. They have been fine marshals and I believe their presence has prevented more than one drunken cowboy from trying to settle his argument with guns or knives."

"You have heard testimony that there has been a systematic

pattern of mistreatment against the ranchers and their riders,'' Henson asked. ''It is true, is it not, that Ike Kramer has spent at least six nights in jail since the Coulters pinned on their badges?''

''Yes. At least six nights.''

''And the McHenrys at least five?''

''Yes.''

''In your opinion, Mr. Mayor, does that validate Mr. Pratt's contention that he was picking on them?''

''No, sir, it does not,'' Malone answered. ''In every case, the Coulters showed amazing forbearance. On more than one of those occasions, a less confident law enforcement officer might have felt a need to resort to guns. The Coulters did not.''

Sam Norton, the bartender of the Red Bull, testified that on the night Win shot Blanchard in the foot, Blanchard had been menacing the entire saloon with a loaded weapon, all the more frightening because he was the only one armed that night, due to a one-night-only ordinance prohibiting the carrying of guns. He had also threatened to kill Muñoz on that night.

Finally, Henson had six witnesses from the saloon who testified that Win had no choice but to shoot Blanchard on the night he was killed. All six swore that Win had given Blanchard an opportunity to surrender but that Blanchard had pulled his gun and shot, even managing to get off the first shot before Win killed him.

''If Marshal Coulter had not turned sideways like he done, that bullet woulda kilt him sure,'' one of the witnesses said.

When the final witness's testimony was heard, Henson walked over to face the jurors. The lawyer turned and pointed to Win and Joe.

''We have asked these men to stand between us and those who would rob us, beat us, and kill us,'' he said. ''The prosecutor has painted a picture that is totally false. He claims that Win and Joe Coulter harassed, abused, and mistreated Ike Kramer and Jim and Frank McHenry, who were nothing more than defenseless cattlemen.

''But I would point out to you that these same 'defenseless' cattlemen killed Kyle Rawlings and five of his riders in a deadly night gun battle. And I would also point out to you that Billy Kramer, Ike's own brother and one of the cattlemen with whom Pratt claims the Coulters have an ongoing feud, has never been arrested or harassed in any way. Why is this? Because Billy Kramer has not violated any laws or ordinances.

"Ike Kramer, Jim and Frank McHenry, and yes, Asa Blanchard were frequent violators of laws, ordinances, and just plain common decency. If that put them at odds with Marshals Win and Joe Coulter, then that is as it should be, for such was the task we as citizens laid out for them to perform.

"It was not some blood lust, then, that brought about the fatal confrontation in the Red Bull Saloon that night. It was, quite simply, a brave man's performance of duty."

Win and Joe both nodded at Henson when he sat down, indicating that they appreciated what he had said and done for them.

Now Pratt rose from his seat. He opened his watch, looked at it, then snapped it shut and put it back into his vest pocket.

"I submit to you, gentlemen of the jury, that every man has his breaking point. The weakest and the most cowardly among us can be pushed to a point at which we will turn and fight. Asa Blanchard was not weak or cowardly, but he was foolish. He was foolish to let a professional gunman goad him into drawing against him.

"I have done some research on these men whom you have hired as your town marshals. During the war they rode not under the Stars and Stripes of the United States, nor even under the Stars and Bars of the Confederacy. Instead, they chose to give their allegiance to the black flag of Quantrill. It is not known how many men they killed during that war, though an estimate of twenty apiece would not be out of hand. Since then they have cut a swath of death and destruction across the Southwest, killing, robbing, and staying just ahead of the wanted posters until they arrived here, where their crimes had not yet caught up with them.

"How many men had Asa Blanchard killed? The answer, my friends is one, and one only. He killed, in an act of understandable rage, the monster who killed Miss Maggie DeShay and at least four young Mexican women before her. Although Muñoz was Mexican, even among his own people he was referred to as *El Bestia*, or 'The Beast.' Had Blanchard not killed Muñoz, it is for sure and certain that a legally constituted court would have sentenced Muñoz to death. Blanchard's killing of Muñoz was wrong then, not because of the act, but because of the timing.

"And finally, I ask you to consider the testimony of the defense's own witnesses. They testified that Blanchard fired first, and we will concede that. He fired first in reaction to the sure and certain knowledge that Win Coulter was going to kill him. Consider the picture their witnesses painted for you. Blanchard, terrified, fires first, his bullet going wide of the mark. Win Coulter, calm, collected, and cold-blooded, stands unflinching in the face of Asa Blanchard's blazing pistol and returns fire. It takes but one shot and Blanchard is dead.

"One shot and Charley Pearl is dead.

"One shot and Vernon Mathis is dead.

"Was it really self-defense as the defendant claims? Or was it a cold, calculated murder, the result of intentionally goading the victim into his irrational reaction?"

"He's good," Doc said in unabashed admiration for the prosecutor. "I've never in my life heard anyone who could do such a good job of turning a heroic action into cold-blooded murder."

"Oh, Doc!" Katie said. "You don't think they will find Win and Joe guilty, do you?"

Doc chuckled. "No. There is an old adage among lawyers: 'When you have evidence, use evidence. When you don't have evidence, use fancy words.' Fancy words are all he had."

"I hope and pray that you are right," Katie said.

The jury deliberated for twenty minutes; then someone saw them leave the deliberation room and shouted to the others. "The jury is comin' back!"

The jury filed in and sat down, trying not to give away the decision by the expressions on their faces. Judge Spicer returned to the court and called it to order.

"Mr. Foreman, have you reached a verdict?"

"We have, Your Honor."

"Would the defendants and their counsel please stand?"

Win, Joe, and Hanson stood. Behind them, Win could hear

the collective pause of breath while the gallery waited.

"What is your verdict?" Judge Spicer asked.

The foreman looked directly at Win and Joe.

"We find the defendants, Win Coulter and Joe Coulter . . . not guilty," the foreman said.

"Good job, Henson!" Doc shouted from the gallery. The court exploded into shouts, some of joy, some of anger. Katie, Suzie, and Doc pushed through the rail to reach them and Doc shook their hands, then stepped back, smiling, as Katie and Suzie gave them much more personal congratulations.

"Coulter!" Ike shouted from the other side of the courtroom.

Win and Joe both looked toward Ike.

"It ain't over, Coulter!" Ike said, pointing menacingly toward them. "It ain't over!"

16

IKE KRAMER TOOK A ROOM AT THE HOMESTEAD HOTEL, BUT he needn't have bothered. The only bed he saw that night was that of one of the crib whores, and that bed wasn't for sleeping.

After Ike left the whore's bed, he decided to make a long, sodden night of it; he sat at a table in the back of the Red Bull sullenly downing shot after shot of whiskey until well past midnight.

At around one o'clock in the morning he decided to get something to eat. The lunchroom he chose happened to be occupied by Win and Joe Coulter, but they didn't seem to notice him. He chose a table in the back and ordered a fried ham sandwich.

About halfway through his sandwich, Doc Masters came in, saw Ike, and went over to his table. "You son of a bitch, you tried to railroad two good men," Doc said angrily. "Pull your gun."

"I've got no quarrel with you."

"Well I've got one with you, you back-shooting bastard!" Doc said. "The Coulters are my friends and you tried to do them in."

Win heard the commotion and looked over.

"Doc," he called easily. "Let him be."

"I'll let him be," Doc said. "When he's six feet under, I'll let him be."

"I said let him be," Win said again, and Doc, still muttering, left the café.

"That man's crazy," Ike said. "Someone ought to lock him up."

"Ike, why don't you finish your sandwich and go on to bed before there's trouble?" Win suggested.

"I'll go where I damn well please," Ike replied.

After the meal Ike left the café, not to go to bed, but to return to the Red Bull Saloon. He drank right through until sunrise the next day.

The next morning, out at the Kramer ranch, Billy went into the dining room for breakfast. The cook had already started the coffee, and its rich aroma filled the kitchen. Billy wandered into the kitchen and poured himself a cup, then leaned against the sideboard, drinking the coffee and watching the cook prepare breakfast.

"Ike up yet?" Billy asked.

"Your brother no come home last night," the Mexican cook said.

"He didn't come home? Are you sure?"

"*Sí*, I am sure. I go into his room to tell him that soon, breakfast will be ready, but he is not in his room and his bed is not . . ." She made a rotary motion with her hand to indicate that the bed had not been mussed.

Billy picked up a golden-brown biscuit from a pan and took a bite from it.

"Then I guess I'd better go into town and see if I can find him, before he gets into trouble," he said. "If it's not already too late."

"I know you're always the one who wants to move on and I'm the one who gets a hankering to stay," Joe said to Win. "But I tell you true, Big Brother, I've about had it with this place."

The two brothers had just finished breakfast and were walking back to the marshal's office.

"I know you're feeling bad about Maggie," Win said. "And ordinarily, I'd be agreeing with you. But I'd sort of hate to leave the town in the lurch right now, especially after the way they all stood up for us at that trial.''

"Well, I can see that. The thing I'm wonderin' is, just how long are you planning on stayin' around?''

"I don't know,'' Win answered. "But I don't think it will be much longer. I got a feeling things will be coming to a head around here soon.''

"You're talking about Kramer and the McHenrys, aren't you?''

"Yes,'' Win answered. "We can't leave now, Joe. Not with this situation unsettled. It would be like running away and it would haunt us both, for the rest of our lives.''

"Yeah,'' Joe said. "I reckon there's some truth to that.''

When they reached the marshal's office, they saw a Mexican standing just outside the door, holding his sombrero in his hand.

"Are you waiting to see us?'' Win asked.

"*Sí,* Señor Marshal.''

"Well, come on in, have a seat,'' Win invited, opening the door and making a motion with his hand. The Mexican, looking around nervously, stepped through the front door. He didn't sit until he was specifically invited to do so.

"Now, what can we do for you?'' Win asked.

"My name is Bustamante, *señor.* Ricardo Bustamante,'' the Mexican said. "Señor Muñoz? He was my cousin.''

"Muñoz was a good man,'' Win said.

"Would you like a cup of coffee?'' Joe asked, gesturing toward the coffeepot.

"No, *gracias, señor.*''

"Bustamante, I'm real sorry about what happened to your cousin,'' Joe said. "I really liked that fella, and I don't believe for a moment that he was the one you folks were calling *El Bestia.*''

"I know now that there is no *El Bestia,*'' Bustamante said.

"What do you mean? Those women were killed,'' Win said.

"*Sí,* and for a while we thought that perhaps the one who was killing was a monster, half man and half animal. We called such a creature *El Bestia.* This is a story that will frighten children, but it is not true. The real murderer is a man, nothing more and nothing less.''

"You say *is* a man, and not *was*," Win said, picking up on the words. "That means you don't believe Muñoz was the one, either."

"No, *señor*. The evil one who did this still lives." Bustamante took a deep breath and looked closely into the faces of the two marshals before he continued. "And I know who he is," he added.

"You know who he is?" Joe asked.

"*Sí, señor*. He is one of you."

"One of us? You mean an American?"

"An American, *sí*." Bustamante pointed to the star on Joe's chest. "But he is also one of *you*. A *guardia*, a lawman. It is Deputy Taggart."

"What?" Win asked. "How do you know?"

"All the *putas* know of Deputy Taggart," Bustamante explained. "Always he has come to the *barrio* for his women, and he takes them but does not pay them. On the night the young girl, Carmelita, was killed, Taggart was first with her *madre*."

"Yeah, but that doesn't prove anything," Win said.

"There is another thing, *señor*. When I thought it was *El Bestia* doing this thing I told Deputy Taggart that anyone who wore a cross would be safe. He laughed and said that Maria Sanchez was wearing a cross and it did not save her."

"Was she?"

"She was not wearing a cross when she was found, *señor*," Bustamante said. "But all who know her say that she always wore the cross given her by her *madre*. The cross cannot be found."

"I'll bet Taggart took the cross," Joe said.

"That is, if he did it," Win replied.

"Shit, you know he did, Win. Taggart is just the kind of lowlife son of a bitch who would do something like that," Joe said. "And if he did do it, that means he killed Maggie too."

When Billy arrived in Epitaph that morning he stopped in front of the general store, where he saw the proprietor sweeping off the store's front porch.

"Have you seen my brother, Mr. Moore?" he asked.

"Not since yesterday, Billy," Moore answered. "I'm sorry."

"Thanks anyway. I'll find him."

Billy tied off his horse and started walking toward the Homestead Hotel.

"Mornin', Billy," someone said as he passed Billy on the board walk.

"Good mornin' to you," Billy said. "Say, have you seen Ike this morning?"

"Matter of fact, I have," the passerby said. "He's over at the Alhambra, having his breakfast."

"Thanks," Billy said.

Billy left the sidewalk and crossed the dirt street, picking his way gingerly through the horse droppings. He pushed the door open at the Alhambra Café and saw Ike sitting at a table in the back. It was all Ike could do to hold his head up. Billy walked back to the table and sat down.

"Billy boy," Ike said, grinning broadly. "I knew you'd come. I knew you wouldn't let your old brother down."

"Look at you," Billy said. "Did you even go to bed last night?"

"Last night?" Ike said. He hiccupped, then smiled. "Last night ain't over yet." He pointed toward the front window. "Oh, it might be light out, but the night ain't over till it's over, if you know what I mean."

"You're so damn drunk I don't think *you* even know what you mean," Billy said.

The waitress brought a plate of eggs, potatoes, and fried ham and set it before Ike. Ike looked at it stupidly for a moment, as if having difficulty making his eyes focus. Then he smiled.

"Oh, yeah," he said, grinning. "I was sitting here waitin' on another drink, but I must've ordered breakfast by mistake." He looked at Billy. "Want some?"

"I ate at home."

"Oh, yeah, I forgot," Ike said. "You're the good boy." Ike put a forkful of eggs into his mouth, and the yellow dribbled down his chin and dripped onto his shirt. His shirt was already stained with whiskey, perfume, powder, and rouge from his night of carousing. "I remember before Pa and Sally died. They both thought I should be more like you. Tell me, Billy, do you think I should be more like you?"

"Would it do any good if I said I thought you should?"

"It might," Ike said. "Course, first I got me this little score to settle with the Coulters. But you know that, 'cause you come to town to help me out."

"Ike, come on," Billy said. "Let's go back home."

"I'll go back after I've settled accounts with the Coulters," Ike said.

"Let it be, Ike. They had their day in court and it's all over now. We've got more important things to worry about than the Coulters."

"No!" Ike shouted. He stood up and leaned over the table, using his fork to point at Billy. The others in the restaurant looked over nervously.

"Ike, sit down," Billy said quietly.

To Billy's surprise, Ike did sit down. But he didn't quit talking. "There ain't nothin' more important than standin' up like a man," he said. "You hear me, Billy? Now, what's it goin' to be? Are you goin' to stand up like a man? Or are you goin' to turn coward and run?"

"Ike, I don't have a quarrel with the Coulters."

"Well, by God I do!" Ike said. "And if you're really my brother . . . my fight is your fight."

"Let it go, Ike."

"No!" Ike shouted, slamming his fist onto the table with such force that his knife and fork bounced onto the floor.

"You're making a scene," Billy cautioned.

"I don't care. This here thing with the Coulters has gone far enough. We're goin' to settle it today, once and for all."

"You aren't in any condition to settle anything," Billy said. "Look at you. Hell, you can't even stand up."

"If the Coulters call me out today, are you goin' to back me up? Or are you goin' to turn tail and run?"

"It won't come to that."

Ike pulled himself together and stared intently into Billy's face. "It might. They're killers, Billy, both of them. You heard what they said about them in court. They rode with Quantrill. No tellin' how many men they kilt when they was with Quantrill. Hell, there's no tellin' how many men they've kilt since then. They might call me out. And if they do, Billy, what I want to know is, will you back me up?''

Billy sighed. "You're my brother, Ike. Of course if it comes to that I will back you up."

Ike grinned broadly. "I was hopin' you'd say that," he said. "Just knowin' I can count on you makes me happy." He put his arm around Billy's shoulder and started for the door. "Come on."

"Where are we going?"

"We're goin' home," Ike said. He laughed. "If the Coulters want to have a shootout, why, they can just have it amongst themselves."

Billy laughed happily. "Now you're making sense."

The sheriff's office was located at the opposite end of Front Street from the marshal's office. Bean looked up when Win and Joe came in.

"Well, what do we have here?" Bean asked. "Town marshals in a county law officer's office. Come to make up, have you?"

"We've come to talk to Taggart," Joe said. "Do you know where he is?"

"He said he had an errand to run," Bean replied. "What do you want with him?"

"I want to arrest him for murder," Win said.

Bean sighed and shook his head, then began drumming his fingers on his desk. He looked up at Win and Joe.

"So, you've come to arrest Taggart for murder," he said. "All right, I see how it is. You figure that we arrested you, so now you are going to have to arrest one of us. Then what, we arrest you again? Look, we can't keep going on like this forever. I'm ready to call it quits, if you two are."

"That's not it, Sheriff," Joe said. "Taggart really is a murderer."

"He is, huh? And just who do you think he murdered?" The inflection in his voice and the expression on his face showed that he was both irritated and unconvinced.

"It wasn't Muñoz who murdered those Mexican whores," Joe said. "It was Deekus Taggart. He also murdered Maggie DeShay."

Now the expression on Bean's face changed, and for just a moment, Win thought he could see belief in the sheriff's eyes.

"Why do you say that?" he asked. The remark wasn't challenging; it appeared to be a genuine request for information. "What I mean is, can you prove it?"

"Well, I'll be damned," Win said. "You suspect him too, don't you?"

"Tell me what you have," Bean said, without answering Win's question.

Win filled him in on the information he and Joe had been given by Bustamante.

"So the big question is, how did Taggart know about that cross?" Win concluded. "Now, you tell me why you have been suspecting him . . . and more important, why you haven't done anything to stop him."

"I have no proof that he has done anything," Bean answered. "I don't even have a real feeling that he has. All I know is, he does like the Mexican women. He goes down there a lot. Or at least, he used to. As far as I know, he hasn't gone down there in a while."

"It's because they're on the lookout for him now," Joe said.

Sheriff Bean shook his head. "No, it can't be Deekus Taggart. Hell, I've known Taggart for years. I think I would know if he was that kind of man."

"Hell, I've only known the son of a bitch for a few weeks, and I know he's like that," Joe said.

"Where does he live?" Win asked.

"Why, he lives right here," Bean said. He pointed toward the back of the office. "There's a room back there. It's really supposed to be for the sheriff, but since I've got my own house, I let him live there. The county pays for it and it saves him a little money."

"Do you mind if we take a look around in his room to see what we might find?" Win asked.

"Oh, I don't know," Bean answered, stroking his chin. "I mean, I wouldn't really want to invade another man's privacy like that. Not without a warrant and all."

"Do you think Taggart did it?" Win asked.

"No, I don't. He's an odd man in some ways, but I just can't believe he would do something like that."

"All right, then look at it this way," Win said. "If we get a warrant, we'll have to tell the judge why we want it. That means it will get out that we suspect Taggart. If Taggart really is innocent like you think he is, the very fact that we suspect him could prejudice other folks against him. But if we do it my way, we can find out one way or the other, and if he's innocent, then no one would be the wiser."

"Yeah," Bean agreed. "I guess you have a point."

"On the other hand, if the son of a bitch *is* guilty, which I think he is, then he doesn't deserve a warrant," Joe said, bitterly.

Taggart's room was locked, but Bean knew there was an extra key in Taggart's desk, so he got it and used it to open the door. It was an unprepossessing room with a bed, a small table and chair, and a trunk. Win opened the trunk and looked through it, but found nothing but clothes.

"See, there's nothing here," Bean said. "What do you say we leave before Taggart gets back and we have to explain ourselves? What did you expect to find, anyway?"

"Maybe this," Joe said. He had just knelt down to look under the bed, and now he dragged out a small wooden box.

"What do you have there, Joe?" Win asked.

"It's just a box," Bean said. "I can't see as it would be of much attention to us."

"Why don't we just see what's in it?" Joe suggested. He opened the box and looked inside. "Son of a bitch," he said.

"What is it, Joe?"

Joe pulled out an ivory cameo brooch. "This was Maggie's. I've seen it on her a dozen times."

"Anything else in there?" Win asked.

"Yeah, I'd say so," Joe said. Reaching down into the box, he wrapped his hand around a gold chain and cross and he held it up. "This is what Bustamante told us about. I'd be willing to bet this belonged to the Sanchez woman.''

Win took out the remaining contents: a small dress, the bracelets, and a string of colored beads. ''And these things belonged to the others,'' he said.

''What do you think now, Sheriff?'' Joe asked.

Bean shook his head, slowly. ''I think you've got the bastard cold,'' he agreed.

17

Taggart had been over to the boot repair shop to get a new heel put on his spare pair of boots and was now bringing them back home. Because the repair shop was on the street behind Front Street, he had taken a shortcut back to his room by cutting through the alley, something he did frequently. Thus he just happened to be passing by the back window of his apartment when he saw someone inside.

At first he thought someone was trying to rob him, and he slipped his pistol out of the holster, then stepped up to the wall and peered through the window for a closer look. That was when he saw Sheriff Bean and the Coulters looking through his box. He had been discovered!

Taggart felt his knees grow weak and he had to put his hand on the wall to keep from falling. His hands started trembling and he was having trouble breathing. What would he do? If it had just been the Coulters, he could deny everything. But Bean was in there too.

Wait. What if he told Bean that it was the Coulters, and that they planted that stuff there to frame him? Yes, that's what he would do. He started toward the front, practicing his story, then he stopped.

What if Bean didn't believe him? There was only one of him, and there were two Coulters. It would be two against one.

Unless the Coulters were gone.

That was it! If the Coulters were dead it would be his word against nobody's word. And if he didn't do it again, ever, then everyone would believe him because the murders would be stopped.

Taggart had seen Ike and Billy in the restaurant a little earlier, and he knew that the McHenrys were down at the Jingle Bell Corral. Everyone knew that a showdown was coming between the Coulters and the cowboys anyway. Why not now?

Putting his boots down in the alley, Taggart hurried down the alley to the back of the Alhambra. Then he ran alongside the building and out into Front Street, where he saw Billy and Ike. Billy was leading his horse and Ike was walking alongside, heading for the Jingle Bell Corral, where he had put up his horse for the night.

"Wait!" Taggart shouted, holding out his hand to stop them. He was badly out of breath from the run and leaned against the wall, his chest heaving, as he breathed in ragged gasps.

"Well, if it isn't my friend Deekus Taggart," Ike said. When he saw how out of breath Taggart was, he walked back toward him. "What the hell is wrong with you?" he asked. "Why are you so out of breath?"

"I had to run to catch you in time to warn you," Taggart said.

"Warn me about what?"

"The Coulters. They're going to be waiting for you boys when you leave town today," Taggart said. "They're telling it all over that they intend to end this feud between you, once and for all. They're going to bushwhack you."

"By God, I can believe that," Ike said. "Bushwhackers they were, and bushwhackers they are." He turned to look toward his brother. "Did you hear that, Billy? Now what do you think?"

"Come on, Ike, let's get out of here," Billy said.

"No! Hell, no! You said if the time ever came you'd be standin' beside me," Ike said. He walked back over to Billy and held his finger in Billy's face. "Well, brother, it's down to the nut-cutting," he said. "The time is here, now."

"Ike, do you know what you're talking about here? You're

talking about going up against men who can kill as easily as they sneeze. We aren't like them."

"You, maybe. You've never killed anyone," Ike said. "But I have. And believe me, Little Brother, there's nothing to it. It ain't the big thing it's made out to be."

Billy swallowed. "All right," he said. "I told you I'd be there for you, and I will be."

"It's not going to be as hard as you think," Ike said. "Jim and Frank have been waitin' for this opportunity. They're in town. We'll get them first, then we'll get this thing settled. There will be four of us and two of them. I think we'll be all right."

"There will be five of us," Taggart said.

Ike and Billy looked at Taggart in surprise. "Five of us?" Ike asked.

Taggart nodded. "I consider you boys my friends," he said. "When the shootin' starts, I plan to be there."

Ike smiled broadly, and reached out to take Taggart's hand. "You're a good man, Deekus," he said. "I always knew that."

"If you want my opinion, I think we should just go home," Frank McHenry said when Ike, Billy, and Taggart found them and told them that they planned to settle this today, once and for all. They were holding the conversation around the watering trough out front of the barn at Jingle Bell Corral. Both the front and back doors of the barn were open to allow air in to cool the horses. Right now a light breeze was blowing through from the opposite side of the barn with the result that it carried on its breath the sweetly pungent smell of horses and manure.

To the right of the door were parked the half-dozen buckboards and wagons the stable had for rent. The stable owner, a man everyone called Muley, was working on the wheel of one of the wagons, though he was far enough away from the five men that he couldn't hear what they were discussing.

"We can't go home, Frank," Jim said. "Ike is right. We've got to have this thing out now. If we don't, we ain't ever goin' to have any peace around here."

"Yeah, well, if we go up against the Coulters we'll have

peace all right. But the only peace some of us are going to have is eternal peace," Frank said. He looked at Billy. "Billy, you're generally the sanest one of us all. I can't believe you're ready for this."

"I don't want it," Billy said. He sighed. "But I'm afraid it's gone too far now. Taggart overheard them planning to ambush us when we leave town. The day I've been dreading is here, and there's nothing we can do about it but play it out."

"Damn," Frank said. Suddenly, and incongruously, he laughed.

"What is it?" Jim asked. "What are you laughin' at?"

"Peaches."

"Peaches?"

"That can of peaches I near about bought a while ago? I wish now I had bought it."

"Why?"

" 'Cause I really love canned peaches, and it mighta been my last chance to ever have any," Frank said. "I don't figure the devil will be servin' 'em in hell."

They were quiet for a moment, then Ike growled. "We goin' to stand around and talk all day? Or are we goin' to get this thing done?"

"Let's get it done," Jim said.

"Wait," Billy called. The others turned to look at him.

"If we're goin' to do this, let's make them come to us," he suggested. "That way, we'll have the advantage. And when it's over, there won't be no question about it bein' murder or anything."

"Yeah, good idea," Ike said. "Muley," he called.

Responding to the call, Muley got up from the wagon wheel and walked over toward them, wiping his hands with a rag he carried in his back pocket.

"Yes, Mr. Kramer?"

"Muley, we want you to do something for us," Ike said. As he was talking, he took out his pistol and began checking the loads in the cylinder. That reminded the others of the necessity of being prepared, so they did the same thing.

"What?" Muley asked, his eyes growing wide at the sight

of five men checking their pistols. "What's going on here?"

"We're about to settle accounts," Ike said. "We want you to go down to the marshal's office and tell them we're waitin' for 'em down here."

"You're going to shoot it out with the Coulters?"

"That's right," Ike said.

Muley shook his head. "You boys don't really want to do that," he said, his voice high-pitched and nervous.

"Yeah," Ike said, looking pointedly at him. "We do. Now, you go down there and get them like we said. Then you stay the hell out of the way."

"And tell the others to stay away too," Billy said. "No need to get any innocent people killed."

Jim laughed. "Your brother's just real thoughtful, ain't he?" he said.

"Yeah," Ike replied, laughing with him. "Like there really was any innocent people in this asshole of a town."

Win and Joe were halfway back to their own office when Muley caught up with them.

"Marshal! It's the Kramers and the McHenrys," he said, excitedly. "They're down at the corral waitin' for you."

"Waiting for us?" Joe asked, the inflection of his voice showing that he was confused by the remark.

Muley nodded. "They're wantin' to shoot it out with you," he said.

"Are they now?" Win replied.

Muley nodded. "Yes, sir. And Deputy Taggart? He's with them too."

Joe grinned, broadly. "Taggart too? Well, what do you know, Win?" he said. "We must've been livin' right. Christmas is comin' early this year."

Win and Joe pulled their guns and checked the loads, then replaced them loosely in the holsters.

"A shootout!" Muley shouted then, running down the street. "The Coulters, the Kramers, and the McHenrys are going to shoot it out!"

Muley's shouts were picked up by others, so that soon people were pouring out into the street from all the stores and houses.

One of those who came outside didn't do so just to watch. Doc Masters came to join in, and he moved out into the middle of the street to walk alongside Win and Joe.

"Doc, this isn't your fight," Win said.

Doc looked hurt, as if the Coulters were going to dinner and he hadn't been invited.

"That's a hell of a thing for you to say to me," Doc replied. "Are you telling me you don't want my help?"

Win looked at Doc, who was nattily dressed as always. "All right," he said. "Raise your right hand."

Doc did so.

"You're deputized," Win said.

"A lawman," Doc said with a little laugh. "This could be the start of a whole new career." Doc broke out into a spasm of coughing.

"You all right, Doc?" Joe asked.

"Don't you worry about me," Doc replied. "I'll be right here with you."

Two of those in the growing crowd were Katie Skyles and Suzie McGuire. As the Courtesan House was close to the Jingle Bell Corral, it was an easy walk over to a place that gave them a front-row vantage point to the action that was about to take place.

"Billy, no!" Suzie shouted when she saw him standing there with his brother and the others. "Billy, you don't belong there! You're not like them! Leave! If they're crazy enough to get themselves killed, let them!"

Billy heard Suzie's anguished shout and looked over at her with an expression of such finality that it was as if he were already dead.

Katie looked at Billy and the others, then looked down the street toward the three men who were walking, resolutely, toward this rendezvous with destiny. She couldn't see one ounce of emotion in the faces of any of the three. When she looked back toward the five they would be facing, though, she could read their thoughts quite easily. Billy's face showed resignation, while Ike's and the McHenrys' reflected fear and excitement. The foolish bravado of Ike and the McHenrys would be no match for the cool courage of the Coulters, Katie thought.

Deekus Taggart, who was standing with them, showed only fear.

Sheriff Bean suddenly appeared, stepping out into the street. He held his hand up to stop Win and the other two.

"Look, boys, we've had our differences," he said. "But this is no way to handle it."

"Bean, they're the ones who sent word to settle it," Win replied. "I figure if it doesn't happen now, while we're facing them, it could happen later when we're not looking."

"Taggart is with them," Joe said.

"That's what I mean. Taggart is my responsibility."

"You're welcome to throw in with us, Sheriff," Doc suggested.

Bean looked at the three men for a moment; then, shaking his head, he stepped back out of the street. "No," he said. "You boys are on your own now. I wash my hands of it."

Doc chuckled. "Why not?" he asked. "It worked for Pontius Pilate."

For a moment, Katie had harbored the irrational thought that perhaps Sheriff Bean could stop the fight. Now she knew with certainty that it was going to take place. Nothing on earth could stop the killing that was about to happen, and she felt her heart go to her throat. She raised her hand to her mouth and watched, numbed with fear.

As Win, Joe, and Doc drew nearer, Billy, Ike, the two McHenrys, and Taggart stepped out in front of the barn, in a little open lot.

Finally the two parties of men faced each other, standing no more then ten feet apart. Taggart, the Kramers, and the McHenrys were now boxed in, for the Coulters and Doc were standing in the open place toward the street. A house blocked one side and a boot repair shop the other. Only the open door of the barn behind them offered any means of escape.

There was a moment of silence as the men confronted each other. Then Win spoke.

"All right, Ike, this is your party," he said. "We're going to give you the first dance."

Jim McHenry made the first move. "You son of a bitch!" he shouted as he reached for his .45.

"No!" Taggart suddenly shouted, throwing his gun down. He took a couple of hesitant steps backward. "No, wait! We'll be killed!" Taggart turned and ran through the open door of the barn behind them. "No, don't shoot us, don't shoot us!" he begged.

"Taggart, you lily-livered coward!" Billy shouted.

Katie saw Billy aim at Win, holding his gun at arm's length. There was something unreal about it, as if she were watching a drama on stage. But Win, who was the most skilled of all of them, had his gun out as quickly as any of them, and the first shot came from Win's gun.

Despite the fact that Billy was aiming at Win, Win concentrated his aim on Ike, for Ike was known to be the best shot of the four remaining men. Katie heard the boom and saw the recoil kick Win's hand up, and she saw the great puff of smoke from the discharge. She heard Ike call out in pain, then she saw him grab his stomach as blood spilled between his fingers. Ike went down. At the same time that Win shot Ike, Joe shot Frank, hitting him in the chest. Billy fired at Win, but missed.

After that, guns began to roar in rapid succession. The next person to be hit was Billy. A bullet from Doc's pistol tore through Billy's right hand. Another hit him in the chest.

"Billy!" Suzie screamed.

Billy staggered back against a window of the vacant house, then slid slowly to the ground. He switched his pistol to his left hand. Sitting there on the ground with his legs crossed, resting his pistol on his shattered arm, he shot with his left hand. His bullet caught Doc between the eyes and Doc went down. Joe shot Billy again, this time in the lower ribs.

"Billy, oh my God!" Suzie cried.

Out of the corner of her eye, Katie could see Taggart running toward the railroad track, heading for the Mexican side of town.

Jim McHenry was the only challenger left standing and he drew blood from Joe, hitting him in the left shoulder. Joe and Win both returned fire at the same time and their bullets slammed into his chest. Jim stumbled out into the street and lurched over toward the people who had crowded around to watch. Unable to shoot for fear of hitting someone in the crowd, Win and Joe both held their fire.

Jim grabbed onto the post that supported the roof over the boot repair shop. Katie and Suzie were standing on that same porch so that, for a moment, Katie was close enough to him to reach out and touch him. Inexplicably, Jim smiled at her before he fell back, dead in the dirt.

Now, only Billy was left alive. He had been knocked flat on his back by Win's last shot, but had managed to work himself upright again. He aimed his pistol at Win and pulled the trigger. The hammer fell on an empty cylinder.

Billy kept pulling the trigger over and over again, but by now the last shot of the fight had been fired, and there remained only the echoes from the distant hills and the *click, click, click* of metal on metal as the hammer of Billy's gun kept falling on empty chambers.

Win stood there watching Billy as he worked the gun. Of all those who had begun the fight, only Win was still standing unscathed. Joe was wounded and Doc was dead. Ike Kramer and Jim and Frank McHenry were dead, and Billy was dying.

"Give it up, Billy," Win said quietly.

Now that the gunfire had died, Suzie jumped down from the porch of the boot repair shop and ran over to Billy. She got down on her knees beside him and took his gun from him.

"One more shot, God," Billy said. "Please, one more shot."

"Billy!" Suzie cried. "Oh, Billy, why did you do this? You've always managed to stay out of trouble. Why, now, of all times, did you join with them?"

"I had no choice," Billy answered in a labored voice. "I had to be loyal to my brother."

Katie had come part of the way with Suzie, and she heard Billy's words. Suddenly she remembered the conversation she'd once had with Win about loyalty and she turned to look at him. Win had already put his gun away and was just standing there, looking at Billy with the saddest expression she had ever seen in a man's face.

"Win," Billy called.

Win moved forward. "Yes, Billy?"

"I hope you understand," he said. "We do what we have to do."

"I know," Win said.

Billy took a couple of audible gasps, then the light faded from his eyes.

"No!" Suzie cried. "No, Billy, no!"

Suzie cradled Billy's head in her lap and looked up as the townspeople approached. The fight had been witnessed by scores of people and now Katie could see them looking down at the bodies of the slain, at Suzie, and even at her. None of the townspeople said anything. Their looks weren't of pity, or compassion, or even hate. Most were of morbid curiosity as if they were experiencing a sensual pleasure from being so close to death while avoiding it themselves.

"Did you ever see anythin' like this?" someone asked.

"Never," another answered. "Did you see ol' Taggart ske-daddle? I never seen such a coward."

"It was over in a hurry, wasn't it?" someone asked.

"Thirty-seven seconds," another said, holding a watch in his hand. "I timed it."

Win looked over at Joe, who had stuffed a handkerchief into the bullet hole. "You all right?" he asked.

"Not much to it," Joe answered. "Doc didn't fare so well, though."

"Dead?"

"Yeah."

"It's a shame," Win said. "He was a good man."

Joe started reloading his pistol. "Come on, Big Brother," he said. "We've got one more to go."

"Did you see where he went?"

"You talking about Taggart?" Sam asked. It wasn't until then that Win saw that the bartender was standing in the crowd with the others.

"Damn, Sam, if you're down here, who's minding the bar?" Win asked.

"Don't need anyone," Sam answered, taking in the crowd with a wave of his hand. "Everyone is down here."

"Yeah, we're talking about Taggart," Win said. "Did you see where he went?"

"He ran across the tracks over to the Mexican side," Sam answered.

When Win and Sam crossed the tracks and started down into the *barrio,* they saw a crowd of people gathered in front of the cantina. They were all in one large circle and they seemed to be looking at something on the ground.

"What do you think that is?" Joe asked, pointing toward the crowd.

"I don't know," Win answered. "I just hope that whatever it is, it wasn't such a distraction that no one saw Taggart. I'd hate for the son of a bitch to get away now."

"Yeah, I would too," Joe replied. He saw Bustamante standing on the outside edge of the crowd of people, and he pointed him out to Win. "There's Bustamante. Maybe he saw Taggart."

"Señor Bustamante," Win called.

The Mexican turned toward them. When he saw that Joe had been wounded, he pointed to the wound. "We heard many gunshots a short time ago," he said. "There was a fight?"

"Yes," Win answered. "But one of them got away. Someone you might be interested in."

"Deputy Taggart?" Bustamante asked.

"Yes. He was seen coming this way. Did you see him?"

"*Sí,* I saw him."

"Good. Where did the son of a bitch go?"

"He went to hell, *señor,*" Bustamante said, matter-of-factly.

"What?"

Speaking in Spanish, Bustamante addressed the crowd; responding to whatever he had said, they opened up a pathway to allow Win and Joe to move to the center. There, lying belly up on the ground in front of the cantina, was Deputy Deekus Taggart. His throat was cut from ear to ear, and flies were already swarming around the sticky red puddle of blood spreading out on the dirt below him.

"As I said, *señor*," Bustamante repeated, "he has gone to hell."

Win took off his star and dropped it on the ground alongside Taggart's body. Joe did the same thing. Then the two brothers turned and walked away.

From the creators of Longarm!
BUSHWHACKERS

They were the most brutal gang of cutthroats ever assembled. And during the Civil War, they sought justice outside of the law—paying back every Yankee raid with one of their own. They rode hard, shot straight, and had their way with every willin' woman west of the Mississippi. No man could stop them. No woman could resist them. And no Yankee stood a chance of living when Quantrill's Raiders rode into town...

Win and Joe Coulter become the two most wanted men in the West. And they learn just how sweet—and deadly—revenge could be...

BUSHWHACKERS by B. J. Lanagan
0-515-12102-9/$4.99
BUSHWHACKERS #2: REBEL COUNTY
0-515-12142-8/$4.99
BUSHWHACKERS#3:
THE KILLING EDGE 0-515-12177-0/$4.99
BUSHWHACKERS #4:
THE DYING TOWN 0-515-12232-7/$4.99
BUSHWHACKERS #5:
MEXICAN STANDOFF 0-515-12263-7/$4.99
BUSHWHACKERS #6:
EPITAPH 0-515-12290-4/$4.99

VISIT PENGUIN PUTNAM ONLINE ON THE INTERNET:
http://www.penguinputnam.com

Payable in U.S. funds. No cash accepted. Postage & handling: $1.75 for one book, 75¢ for each additional. Maximum postage $5.50. Prices, postage and handling charges may change without notice. Visa, Amex, MasterCard call 1-800-788-6262, ext. 1, or fax 1-201-933-2316; refer to ad #705

Or,check above books	Bill my: ☐ Visa ☐ MasterCard ☐ Amex _____(expires)
and send this order form to:	
The Berkley Publishing Group	Card#_____
P.O. Box 12289, Dept. B	Daytime Phone #_____ ($10 minimum)
Newark, NJ 07101-5289	Signature_____

Please allow 4-6 weeks for delivery.   Or enclosed is my: ☐ check ☐ money order
Foreign and Canadian delivery 8-12 weeks.

Ship to:

Name_____	Book Total	$_____
Address_____	Applicable Sales Tax (NY, NJ, PA, CA, GST Can.)	$_____
City_____	Postage & Handling	$_____
State/ZIP_____	Total Amount Due	$_____

Bill to: Name_____

Address_____City_____
State/ZIP_____

JAKE LOGAN

TODAY'S HOTTEST ACTION WESTERN!

__SLOCUM AND THE LADY IN BLUE #217   0-515-12049-9/$4.99
__SLOCUM AND THE POWDER RIVER
   GAMBLE #218   0-515-12070-7/$4.99
__SLOCUM AND THE COLORADO
   RIVERBOAT #219   0-515-12081-2/$4.99
__SLOCUM #220: SLOCUM'S INHERITANCE 0-515-12103-7/$4.99
__SLOCUM AND DOC HOLLIDAY #221   0-515-12131-2/$4.99
__SLOCUM AND THE AZTEC PRIESTESS #222 0-515-12143-6/$4.99
__SLOCUM AND THE IRISH LASS (GIANT)   0-515-12155-X/$5.99
__SLOCUM AND THE COMANCHE
   RESCUE #223   0-515-12161-4/$4.99
__SLOCUM #224: LOUISIANA LOVELY   0-515-12176-2/$4.99
__SLOCUM #225: PRAIRIE FIRES   0-515-12190-8/$4.99
__SLOCUM AND THE REAL McCOY #226   0-515-12208-4/$4.99
__SLOCUM #227: BLOOD ON THE BRAZOS 0-515-12229-7/$4.99
__SLOCUM AND THE SCALPLOCK TRAIL #228 0-515-12243-2/$4.99
__SLOCUM AND THE TEXAS ROSE #229   0-515-12264-5/$4.99
__SLOCUM AND THE COMELY CORPSE #230 0-515-12277-7/$4.99
__SLOCUM #231: BLOOD IN KANSAS   0-515-12291-2/$4.99
__SLOCUM AND THE GREAT DIAMOND
   HOAX #232 (7/98)   0-515-12301-3/$4.99

Payable in U.S. funds. No cash accepted. Postage & handling: $1.75 for one book, 75¢ for each additional. Maximum postage $5.50. Prices, postage and handling charges may change without notice. Visa, Amex, MasterCard call 1-800-788-6262, ext. 1, or fax 1-201-933-2316; refer to ad #202d

Or, check above books   Bill my: ☐ Visa ☐ MasterCard ☐ Amex _____ (expires)
and send this order form to:
The Berkley Publishing Group Card#_____
P.O. Box 12289, Dept. B   Daytime Phone #_____ ($10 minimum)
Newark, NJ 07101-5289   Signature_____
Please allow 4-6 weeks for delivery. Or enclosed is my: ☐ check ☐ money order
Foreign and Canadian delivery 8-12 weeks.

Ship to:

Name_____ Book Total $_____
Address_____ Applicable Sales Tax $_____
                            (NY, NJ, PA, CA, GST Can.)
City_____ Postage & Handling $_____
State/ZIP_____ Total Amount Due $_____

Bill to: Name_____

Address_____City_____
State/ZIP_____

J. R. ROBERTS

THE
GUNSMITH

__THE GUNSMITH #187:	LEGBREAKERS AND	
	HEARTBREAKERS	0-515-12105-3/$4.99
__THE GUNSMITH #188:	THE ORIENT EXPRESS	0-515-12133-9/$4.99
__THE GUNSMITH #189:	THE POSSE FROM	
	ELSINORE	0-515-12145-2/$4.99
__THE GUNSMITH #190:	LADY ON THE RUN	0-515-12163-0/$4.99
__THE GUNSMITH #191:	OUTBREAK	0-515-12179-7/$4.99
__THE GUNSMITH #192:	MONEY TOWN	0-515-12192-4/$4.99
__GUNSMITH GIANT #3:	SHOWDOWN AT	
	LITTLE MISERY	0-515-12210-6/$5.99
__THE GUNSMITH #193:	TEXAS WIND	0-515-12231-9/$4.99
__THE GUNSMITH #194:	MASSACRE AT ROCK	
	SPRINGS	0-515-12245-9/$4.99
__THE GUNSMITH #195:	CRIMINAL KIN	0-515-12266-1/$4.99
__THE GUNSMITH #196:	THE COUNTERFEIT	
	CLERGYMAN	0-515-12279-3/$4.99
__THE GUNSMITH #197:	APACHE RAID	0-515-12293-9/$4.99
__THE GUNSMITH #198:	THE LADY KILLERS (7/98)	0-515-12303-X/$4.99

Payable in U.S. funds. No cash accepted. Postage & handling: $1.75 for one book, 75¢ for each additional. Maximum postage $5.50. Prices, postage and handling charges may change without notice. Visa, Amex, MasterCard call 1-800-788-6262, ext. 1, or fax 1-201-933-2316; refer to ad #206g

Or, check above books   Bill my: ☐ Visa ☐ MasterCard ☐ Amex _____ (expires)
and   send   this   order   form   to:
The Berkley Publishing Group   Card# _____
P.O. Box 12289, Dept. B   Daytime Phone # _____ ($10 minimum)
Newark, NJ 07101-5289   Signature _____
Please allow 4-6 weeks for delivery.   Or enclosed is my: ☐ check ☐ money order
Foreign and Canadian delivery 8-12 weeks.

Ship   to:

Name_____	Book Total	$_____
Address_____	Applicable Sales Tax (NY, NJ, PA, CA, GST Can.)	$_____
City_____	Postage & Handling	$_____
State/ZIP_____	Total Amount Due	$_____

Bill   to: Name_____

Address_____City_____

State/ZIP_____

LONGARM

Explore the exciting Old West with one of the men who made it wild!

__LONGARM AND THE BACKWOODS
BARONESS #222   0-515-12080-4/$4.99

__LONGARM AND THE DOUBLE-BARREL
BLOWOUT #223   0-515-12104-5/$4.99

__LONGARM AND THE MAIDEN
MEDUSA #224   0-515-12132-0/$4.99

__LONGARM AND THE DEAD MAN'S PLAY
#225   0-515-12144-4/$4.99

__LONGARM AND THE LADY FAIRE #226   0-515-12162-2/$4.99

__LONGARM AND THE REBEL
EXECUTIONER #227   0-515-12178-9/$4.99

__LONGARM AND THE BORDER WILDCAT #229 0-515-12209-2/$4.99

__LONGARM AND THE WYOMING
WILDWOMEN #230   0-515-12230-0/$4.99

__LONGARM AND THE DURANGO DOUBLE-CROSS
#231   0-515-12244-0/$4.99

__LONGARM AND THE WHISKEY CREEK
WIDOW #232   0-515-12265-3/$4.99

__LONGARM AND THE BRANDED BEAUTY
#233   0-515-12278-5/$4.99

__LONGARM AND THE RENEGADE ASSASSINS
#234   0-515-12292-0/$4.99

__LONGARM AND THE WICKED
SCHOOLMARM #235 (7/98)   0-515-12302-1/$4.99

Payable in U.S. funds. No cash accepted. Postage & handling: $1.75 for one book, 75¢ for each additional. Maximum postage $5.50. Prices, postage and handling charges may change without notice. Visa, Amex, MasterCard call 1-800-788-6262, ext. 1, or fax 1-201-933-2316; refer to ad #201g

| Or, check above books and send this order form to:
The Berkley Publishing Group
P.O. Box 12289, Dept. B
Newark, NJ 07101-5289
Please allow 4-6 weeks for delivery.
Foreign and Canadian delivery 8-12 weeks. | Bill my: ☐ Visa ☐ MasterCard ☐ Amex _____(expires)
Card#_____
Daytime Phone #_____ ($10 minimum)
Signature_____
Or enclosed is my: ☐ check ☐ money order |

Ship to:

Name_____	Book Total	$_____
Address_____	Applicable Sales Tax (NY, NJ, PA, CA, GST Can.)	$_____
City_____	Postage & Handling	$_____
State/ZIP_____	Total Amount Due	$_____

Bill to: Name_____

Address_____City_____

State/ZIP_____